MY SISTER LIVES ON THE MANTELPIECE

Annabel Pitcher

First published in Great Britain in 2011 by Orion
Children's Books, a division of
the Orion Publishing Group Ltd
This Large Print edition published 2012
by AudioGO Ltd
by arrangement with
the Orion Publishing Group Ltd

ISBN: 978 1445 886831

British Library Cataloguing in Publication Data available

Printed and bound in Great Britain by
MPG Books Group Limited

For Mum and Dad, who got me here.

1

My sister Rose lives on the mantelpiece. Well, some of her does. Three of her fingers, her right elbow and her kneecap are buried in a graveyard in London. Mum and Dad had a big argument when the police found ten bits of her body. Mum wanted a grave that she could visit. Dad wanted a cremation and to sprinkle the ashes in the sea. That's what Jasmine told me anyway. She remembers more than I do. I was only five when it happened. Jasmine was ten. She was Rose's twin. Still is, according to Mum and Dad. They dressed Jas the same for years after the funeral—flowery dresses, cardigans, those flat shoes with buckles that Rose used to love. I reckon that's why Mum ran off with the man from the support group seventy one days ago. When Jas cut off all her hair, dyed it pink and got her nose pierced on her fifteenth birthday, she didn't look like Rose any more and my parents couldn't hack it.

They each got five bits. Mum put hers in a fancy white coffin beneath a fancy white headstone that says *My Angel* on it. Dad burned a collarbone, two ribs, a bit of skull and a little toe and put the ashes in a golden urn. So they both got their own way, but surprise surprise it didn't make them happy. Mum says the graveyard's too depressing to visit. And every anniversary Dad tries to sprinkle the ashes but changes his mind at the last minute. Something seems to happen right when Rose is about to be tipped into the sea. One year in Devon there were loads of these swarming silver fish that looked like they couldn't wait to eat my sister. And another year in Cornwall a seagull poohed on the urn just as Dad was about to open it. I started to laugh but Jas looked sad so I stopped.

We moved out of London to get away from it all. Dad knew someone who knew someone who rung him up about a job on a building site in the Lake District. He hadn't worked in London for ages. There's a recession, which means the country has no money, so hardly anything's getting built. When he got the job in Ambleside, we sold our flat and rented a cottage and left Mum in London. I bet Jas five whole pounds that Mum would come to wave us off. She didn't make me pay when I lost. In the car Jas said *Let's play I Spy*, but she couldn't guess *Something beginning with R*, even though Roger was sitting right on my lap, purring as if he was giving her a clue.

It's so different here. There are massive mountains that are tall enough to poke God up the bum, hundreds of trees, and it's quiet. *No people* I said, as we found the cottage down a twisty lane and I looked out of the window for somebody to play with. *No Muslims* Dad corrected me, smiling for the first time that day. Me and Jas didn't smile back as we got out of the car.

Our cottage is the complete opposite of our flat in Finsbury Park. It's white not brown, big not small, old not new. Art's my favourite subject at school and, if I painted the buildings as people, I would turn the cottage into a crazy old granny, smiling with no teeth. The flat would be a serious soldier all smart and squashed up in a row of identical men. Mum would love that. She's a teacher at an art college and I reckon she'd show every single one of her students if I sent her my pictures.

Even though Mum's in London, I was happy to leave the flat behind. My room was tiny but I wasn't allowed to swap with Rose 'cos she's dead and her stuff's sacred. That was the answer I always got whenever I asked if I could move. *Rose's room is sacred, James. Don't go in there, James. It's sacred.* I don't see what's sacred about a bunch of old dolls, a smelly pink duvet and a bald teddy. Didn't feel that sacred when I jumped up and down on Rose's bed one day when I got home from school. Jas made me stop but she promised not to tell.

When we'd got out of the car, we stood and looked at our new home. The sun was setting, the mountains glowed orange and I could see our reflection in one of the cottage windows—Dad, Jas, me holding Roger. For a millisecond I felt hopeful, like this really was the beginning of a brand new life and everything was going to be okay from now on. Dad grabbed a suitcase and the key out of his pocket and walked down the garden path. Jas grinned at me, stroked Roger, then followed. I put the cat down. He crawled straight into a bush, tail sticking out as he scrambled through the leaves. *Come on* Jas called, turning around at the porch door. She held out a hand as I ran to join her. We walked into the cottage together.

*   *   *

Jas saw it first. I felt her arm go stiff. *Do you want a cup of tea* she said, her voice too high and her eyes on something in Dad's hand. He was crouching on the lounge floor, his clothes thrown everywhere as if he'd emptied his suitcase in a rush. *Where's the*

3

kettle she asked, trying to act normal. Dad didn't look up from the urn. He spat on it, polishing the gold with the end of his sleeve 'til it gleamed. Then he put my sister on the mantelpiece, which was cream and dusty and just like the one in the flat in London, and he whispered *Welcome to your new home, sweetheart.*

Jas picked the biggest room. It has an old fireplace in the corner and a built-in wardrobe that she's filled with all her new black clothes. She's hung wind chimes from the beams on the ceiling and they tinkle if you blow on them. I prefer my room. The window overlooks the back garden, which has a creaky apple tree and a pond, and there's this really wide windowsill that Jas put a cushion on. The first night we arrived, we sat on it for ages, staring at the stars. I never saw them in London. All the lights from the buildings and cars made it too bright to see anything in the sky. Here the stars are really clear and Jas told me all about the constellations. She's into horoscopes and reads hers every morning on the Internet. It tells her exactly what's going to happen that day. *Doesn't it spoil the surprise* I asked in London when Jas pretended to be sick 'cos her horoscope said something about an unexpected event. *That's the point* she replied, getting back into bed and pulling the covers over her head.

*　　　*　　　*

Jas is a Gemini, the symbol of the twins, which is strange 'cos she's not a twin any more. I'm a Leo and my symbol is the lion. Jas knelt up on the cushion and pointed at it out of the window. It didn't look much like an animal, but Jas said that

4

whenever I'm upset, I should think of the silver lion above my head and everything will be all right. I wanted to ask why she was saying this stuff when Dad had promised us a Fresh New Start, but I thought of the urn on the mantelpiece and I was too scared of the answer. Next morning, I found an empty vodka bottle in the bin and I knew that life in the Lake District would be exactly the same as life in London.

That was two weeks ago. Since the urn, Dad's unpacked the old photo album and some of his clothes. The removal men did the big stuff like beds and the sofa, and me and Jas did everything else. The only boxes we haven't unpacked are the huge ones marked SACRED. They're in the cellar covered with plastic bags to keep them dry in case there's a flood or something. When we closed the cellar door, Jas's eyes went all damp and smudgy. She said *Doesn't it bother you* and I said *No* and she said *Why not* and I said *Rose is dead.* Jas screwed up her face. *Don't use that word, Jamie.*

I don't see why not. Dead. Dead. Dead dead dead. *Passed away* is what Mum says. *Gone to a better place* is Dad's phrase. He never goes to church so I don't know why he says it. Unless the better place he's talking about is not Heaven but the inside of a coffin or a golden urn.

*   *   *

My counsellor in London said I was *In denial and still suffering from shock.* She said *It will hit you one day and then you will cry.* Apparently I haven't since September 9th almost five years ago, which is when it happened. Last year, Mum and Dad sent me to

5

that fat woman 'cos they thought it was weird that I didn't cry about Rose. I wanted to ask if they'd cry about someone they couldn't remember, but I bit my tongue.

That's the thing no one seems to get. I don't remember Rose. Not really. I remember two girls on holiday playing Jump The Wave, but I don't know where we were, or what Rose said, or if she enjoyed the game. And I know my sisters were bridesmaids at a neighbour's wedding, but all I can picture is the tube of Smarties that Mum gave me during the service. Even then I liked the red ones best and I held them in my hand until they stained my skin pink. But I can't remember what Rose wore, or how she looked walking down the aisle, or anything like that. After the funeral, when I asked Jas where Rose was, she pointed at the urn on the mantelpiece. *How can a girl fit inside something so small* I said, which made Jas cry. That's what she told me anyway. I don't really remember.

One day for homework I had to describe someone special, and I spent fifteen minutes writing a whole page on Wayne Rooney. Mum made me rip it out and write about Rose instead. I had nothing to say so Mum sat opposite me with her face all red and wet and told me exactly what to put. She smiled this teary smile and said *When you were born, Rose pointed at your willy and asked if it was a worm* and I said *I'm not putting that in my English book*. Mum's smile disappeared. Tears dripped off her nose onto her chin and it made me feel bad so I wrote it down. A few days later, the teacher read out my homework in class and I got a gold star from her and teased by everyone else. *Maggot Dick*, they called me.

2

It's my birthday tomorrow and a week after that I start at my new school, Ambleside Church of England Primary. It's about two miles from the cottage so Dad will have to drive. It's not like London here. There are no buses or trains if Dad's too drunk to go out. Jas says she'll walk with me if we can't get a lift as her school is about a mile further on. She said *At least we'll get thin* and I looked at my arms and said *Thin is a bad thing for boys*. Jas doesn't need to lose any weight but she eats like a mouse and spends hours reading the backs of packets looking at the calories. Today she made a cake for my birthday. She said it was a healthy one with margarine not butter and hardly any sugar so it will probably taste funny. Looks good though. We are having it tomorrow and I get to cut it 'cos it's my special day.

I checked the post earlier and there was nothing except a menu from The Curry House, which I hid so Dad wouldn't get angry. No birthday present from Mum. No card. But there's still tomorrow. She won't forget. Before we left London, I bought a We Are Moving House card and sent it to her. All I wrote inside was the cottage's address and my name. I didn't know what else to put. She's living in Hampstead with that man from the support group. His name is Nigel and I met him at one of those memorial things in the centre of London. Long straggly beard. Crooked nose. Smoked a pipe. He writes books about other people who have written books, which I think is pointless. His wife died on

September 9th as well. Maybe Mum'll marry him. Maybe they'll have a baby and call it Rose and then they will forget all about me and Jas and Nigel's first wife. I wonder if he found any bits of her. There might be an urn on his mantelpiece and he might buy it flowers on their wedding anniversary. Mum would hate that.

Roger's just come into my room. He likes to curl up at night by the radiator where it's warm. Roger loves it here. In London he was always kept indoors 'cos of the traffic. Here he can roam free and there are lots of animals to hunt in the garden. On our third morning, I found something small and grey and dead on the doorstep. I think it was a mouse. I couldn't pick it up with my fingers so I got a piece of paper and pushed it on with a stick and then I threw it in the bin. But then I felt mean so I got it out of the bin and put it under the hedge and covered it with grass. Roger meowed as if he couldn't believe what I was doing after all his hard work. I told him that dead things make me sick and he rubbed his orange body on my right shin so I knew he understood. It's true. Dead bodies freak me out. Sounds nasty to say but, if she had to die, I'm glad Rose was found in bits. It would be much worse if she were under the ground, stiff and cold, looking exactly like the girl in the photos.

I suppose my family was happy once. The pictures show lots of big smiles and small eyes, all crinkled up like someone's just told a really good joke. Dad spent hours staring at those photos in London. We had hundreds, all taken before September 9th, and they were in a big jumble in five different boxes. Four years after Rose died, he decided to put them in order, with the oldest last

8

and the most recent first. He bought ten of these really posh albums that are proper leather and have gold writing on them, and he spent every evening for months not speaking to anyone just drinking drinking drinking and gluing all the pictures in the right place. Only the more he drank the less he could stick straight so the next day he would have to do half of them all over again. That's probably when Mum started having The Affair. That was a word I'd heard on Eastenders and not one I expected my own dad to shout. It was a shock. I didn't guess, not even when Mum started going to the support group two times a week, then three times a week, then pretty much whenever she could.

Sometimes when I wake up, I forget that she's gone and then I remember and my heart drops like it does when you miss a step or trip over a kerb. Everything comes rushing back and I can see what happened on Jas's birthday too clearly, as if my brain's one of those HD televisions that Mum said was a waste of money when I asked for one last Christmas.

Jas was an hour late for her party. Mum and Dad were arguing. *Christine told me you weren't with her* Dad said as I walked into the kitchen. *I phoned to check.* Mum sank into a chair right by the sandwiches, which I thought was clever 'cos she'd have first choice of the fillings. There were beef ones and chicken ones and yellow ones that I hoped were cheese not egg mayonnaise. Mum was wearing a party hat but her mouth was droopy so she looked like one of those sad clowns you see at the circus. Dad opened the fridge door, took a beer and slammed it shut. There were already four empty cans on the kitchen table. *So where the hell were you*

9

he said. Mum opened her mouth to speak but my tummy rumbled loudly. She jumped and they both turned to look at me. *Can I have a sausage roll* I asked.

Dad grunted and grabbed a plate. Even though he was angry, he carefully cut a piece of cake, surrounding it with sausage rolls and sandwiches and crisps. He poured a glass of Ribena, making it strong, exactly how I like it. When he'd finished, I held out my hands, but he walked straight past me towards the mantelpiece in the lounge. I was annoyed. Everyone knows that dead sisters don't get hungry. Just as I thought my tummy might eat me alive, the front door swung open. *You're late* Dad shouted but then Mum gasped. Jas smiled nervously, her nose twinkling with a diamond stud and her hair pinker than bubblegum. I smiled back but then BAM there was an explosion as Dad dropped the plate and Mum whispered *What have you done*.

Jas went bright red. Dad shouted something about Rose and pointed at the urn, splashing Ribena all over the carpet. Mum sat still, her eyes on Jas's face as they filled with tears. I stuffed two sausage rolls into my mouth and hid a bun underneath my t-shirt.

Some family Dad spat, looking from Jas to Mum, his face tight with a sadness I didn't understand. It was only a haircut and I couldn't figure out what Mum had done wrong. Roger was licking birthday cake off the carpet. He hissed when Dad grabbed him by the scruff of his neck and threw him into the hall. Jas stormed off and slammed her bedroom door. I managed to eat a sandwich and three more buns as Dad cleaned the mess, his hands trembling as he picked up the remains of Rose's birthday tea. Mum stared at the cake on the carpet. *This is all my fault* she muttered. I shook my head. *He spilt it, not you* I whispered, pointing at the Ribena stain.

Dad threw the food into the bin so hard that it rattled. He started shouting again. It hurt my ears so I ran out of the kitchen into Jas's room. She was sitting in front of the mirror, fiddling with her pink hair. I gave her the bun hidden underneath my top. *You look really nice* I said, which made her cry. Girls are strange.

Mum admitted everything after the party. Me and Jas were on her bed, listening. Wasn't hard. Mum was crying. Dad was screaming. Jas was bawling her eyes out but mine were dry. *AFFAIR* Dad said, over and over again, like if he yelled it enough times then maybe it would sink in. Mum said *You don't understand* and Dad said *I suppose Nigel does* and Mum said *Better than you. We talk. He listens. He makes me*—but Dad interrupted, swearing loudly.

It went on for ages. I got pins and needles in my left foot. Dad asked hundreds of questions. Mum sobbed even harder. He called her *A cheat* and *A liar* and said *This is the icing on the bloody cake*, which made me want another bun. Mum tried to argue back. Dad shouted over her. *Haven't you put this family through enough* he roared. The crying stopped suddenly. Mum said something we couldn't hear. *What* Dad said, shocked. *What did you say.*

Footsteps in the hall. Mum's voice again, quiet, just outside Jas's door. *I can't do this any more* she repeated, sounding a thousand years old. Jas grabbed my hand. *I think it's better if I go.* My fingers ached as Jas squeezed them. *Better for who*

11

Dad asked. *Better for everyone* Mum replied.

It was Dad's turn to cry. He begged Mum to stay. Apologised. He blocked the front door but Mum said *Move out of my way*. Dad asked for one more chance. He promised to try harder, to put the photos away, to get a job. He said *I lost Rose and I can't lose you* as Mum walked out onto the street. Dad shouted *We need you* and Mum said *Not as much as I need Nigel*. And then she left so Dad thumped the wall and broke his finger and he had to wear a bandage for four weeks and three days.

3

The post hasn't arrived. It is thirteen minutes past ten and I have been in double figures for one hundred and ninety seven minutes. I heard something at the door a second ago but it was just the milkman. We had to get our own milk in London. We'd always run out 'cos the supermarket was a fifteen minute drive away and Dad refused to go down the road to the shop owned by Muslims. I got used to having dry cereal but Mum moaned when she couldn't have a cup of tea.

So far my presents haven't been that great. Dad gave me football boots that are one and a half sizes too small. I'm wearing them now and my toes feel as though they're in a mousetrap. First time he's smiled for ages when I put them on. I didn't want to say I needed bigger ones 'cos he probably chucked the receipt. I just pretended that they fit. I never get on football teams anyway so I won't have to wear them that much. In my school in London I tried out every single year but I was never picked, except for once when the keeper was ill and Mr Jackson put me in goal. I asked Dad to come and he rubbed my head like he was proud. We lost thirteen-nil, but only six of the goals were my fault. When the match started, I was gutted Dad hadn't turned up. By the end, I was relieved.

Rose bought me a book. Like always, her present was by the urn when I went into the lounge. I got this strong urge to laugh when I saw it there, and imagined the urn sprouting legs and arms and a head and walking to the shop to buy a present. Dad was watching me with his serious eyes though so I tore off the paper and tried not to look disappointed when I realised I'd already read it. I read a lot. I used to go to the school library at lunchtime in London. *Books are better friends than people* the librarian said. I don't think that's true. Luke Branston was my friend for four days when he fell out with Dillon Sykes for breaking his Arsenal ruler. He sat with me in the dining hall and we played Top Trumps in the playground and no one called me *Maggot Dick* for almost a whole week.

Jas is waiting for me downstairs. We're going to the park to play football in a second. She asked Dad too. *Come and watch Jamie try out his new boots* she said, but Dad just grunted and turned on the TV. He looked hung-over. Sure enough, I found another empty vodka bottle in the bin when I checked. Jas whispered *We don't need him anyway* and then shouted *Let's go and play* as if it was the most exciting thing in the world.

Jas just yelled up the stairs to see if I'm ready. I shouted *Nearly* but I didn't move from the windowsill. I want to wait for the post. It normally comes between ten and eleven. I don't think Mum will forget. Important birthdays feel like they're written on my brain in that permanent ink teachers sometimes use on whiteboards by mistake. But maybe Mum is different now she lives with Nigel. Maybe Nigel has children of his own and Mum remembers their birthdays instead.

I'll definitely get something from Granny even if I don't get anything from Mum. Granny lives in Scotland, which is where Dad is from, and she never forgets anything even though she is eighty one. I wish I could see her more often 'cos she is the only person Dad is scared of and I reckon she is the only one who could make him stop drinking. Dad never takes us to see her and she is too old to drive so she can't visit us. I think I am a lot like Granny. She has ginger hair and freckles and I have ginger hair and freckles and she is tough like me. At Rose's funeral, she was the only other person in the whole church who didn't cry. That's what Jas told me anyway.

*   *   *

The park is a mile away and we almost sprinted there. I could tell Jas was trying to burn calories. Sometimes when we watch TV, she jiggles her leg up and down for no reason and she does hundreds of sit-ups every day after school. She looked funny in her long dark coat with her bright pink hair, speeding past loads of sheep that stared and said *Baaa*. I kept looking for the postman 'cos it was almost eleven and he hadn't arrived by the time we left the cottage.

There were three girls on the swings when we got to the park and they stared at us as we walked

14

in. Their eyes were like nettles, all full of sting, and my face went red as I paused by the gate. Jas wasn't bothered. She ran right up to them and climbed on one of the swings, standing on the seat in her jet black boots. The girls looked at her as though she was a freak, but Jas swung really high and really fast and smiled at the sky like nothing in the world could frighten her.

Music's more Jas's thing so I beat her easily, seven-two. My best goal was a volley with my left foot. Jas reckons I'll get on the team this year. She said my boots are enchanted so they'll make me as good as Wayne Rooney. My toes tingled as if there was magic inside them, and for a second I thought Jas was right until I realised my blood supply had been cut off and my feet had turned blue. Jas said *Are your boots too small* and I said *No they are perfect.*

I felt excited on the way home. Jas was going on and on about getting more piercings but all I could think about was the mat in the hall in the cottage. In my head I saw a parcel on top of it. A fat parcel with a football card taped to the shiny wrapping paper. Nigel wouldn't have signed it but Mum would have put lots of kisses inside.

When I opened the front door, I knew something was wrong. It swung forward easily. I didn't dare look down at first and forced myself to remember what Granny always says. *Good things come in small packages.* I tried to imagine all the little presents Mum could have sent that were still nice even if they didn't block the door. But for some reason the only small thing I could think of was Roger's dead mouse and it made me feel sick so I stopped.

I looked down at the mat. There was one card. I

15

recognised the loopy handwriting on the envelope as Granny's. Even though I could tell there was nothing underneath it, I still nudged the card with my toe, in case the present Mum had sent was really really tiny, like a Manchester United badge or a rubber or something.

I could feel Jas watching me. I glanced up at her. Once I saw a dog run into a busy road and my shoulders shot up to my ears and my eyebrows scrunched together as I waited for the collision. That's how Jas looked when I checked the mat. I bent down quickly and tore open Granny's card, laughing too loudly when twenty pounds fluttered onto the carpet. *Think of all the cool stuff you can buy with your money* Jas said, and I was glad that she hadn't asked me a question 'cos I had a lump the size of the world in my throat.

In the lounge we heard the clunk-fizz of a can being opened and Jas coughed to disguise the fact that Dad was drinking on my special day. *Let's have some cake* she said, pulling me into the kitchen. There weren't any candles so she stuck a couple of her incense sticks into the sponge. I closed my eyes tight and wished that Mum's present would arrive soon. I wished for the biggest parcel in the whole world, one that would break the postman's back. Then I opened my eyes and saw Jas smiling at me. I felt a bit selfish so I added *And please let Jas get her belly button pierced* before taking a deep breath. Smoke went everywhere but it was impossible to blow out the sticks so my wishes won't work.

I cut the cake as carefully as I could 'cos I didn't want to spoil it. It tasted like Yorkshire pudding. *This is really nice* I said and Jas laughed. She knew I was lying. She shouted *Dad, do you want some*

16

but there was no reply. Then she said *Do you feel older* and I said *No* 'cos nothing has changed. Even though I am in double figures now, I still feel like I did when I was nine. I am the same as I was in London. Jas is the same. And so is Dad. He hasn't been to the building site even though the man has left him five answerphone messages in two weeks.

Jas nibbled the corner of a tiny slice of cake and asked if I wanted my present. The wind chimes tinkled as we opened her bedroom door. She said *I didn't wrap it* and handed me a white plastic bag. Inside was a sketchbook and some fancy pencils, the nicest I've ever seen. *I'll draw you first* I said. She stuck out her tongue and went cross-eyed. *Only if you draw me like this.*

After lunch we watched Spider-Man. It is the number one best film of all time and we sat on her bedroom floor with the curtains closed and the duvet wrapped around us, even though it was the middle of the afternoon. Roger curled up on my lap. He's my cat really. I'm the one who looks after him. He used to be Rose's. She begged and begged for a pet and, when she was seven, Mum agreed. She put the cat in a box and stuck a bow on top and when Rose opened the present she cried with happiness. Mum's told me that story about a hundred times. I don't know if she forgets she's told it before, or if she just likes telling it again, but it makes her smile so I just bite my tongue and let her finish. I'd love it if Mum sent me an animal for my birthday. A spider would be best 'cos then it might bite me and I'd get special powers like Spider-Man.

When I went downstairs after the film, almost all the cake had gone. There was just one bit on the plate, but it wasn't a neat triangle like the slices I'd

17

cut. It was all hacked up. I walked into the lounge and found Dad snoring on the sofa with crumbs on his double chin. Three empty beer cans were on the floor and a bottle of vodka was propped against a cushion. He must have been too drunk to realise the cake didn't taste right. I was about to go back upstairs when I caught sight of my sister on the mantelpiece. Next to the urn was a slice of cake and for some reason it made me really cross. I walked over to Rose and, even though I know she's dead and can't hear a word that anyone says, I whispered *It's my birthday, not yours* and stuffed the cake into my mouth.

*   *   *

Two days later, I was in the back garden sketching a goldfish in the pond and trying not to listen out for the postman. I'd told myself again and again that the present wouldn't come but, as soon as I heard footsteps on the drive, I ran inside. A few letters flopped onto the mat. Nothing from Mum. But then there was a knock on the door and I opened it so quickly, the postman jumped. He said *Package for James Matthews* and my hands trembled as I took the parcel. The postman said *Sign here* in this bored voice as if he didn't know that something amazing was happening. Feeling like Wayne Rooney, I signed my name and made it all squiggly like an autograph. Then the postman turned around and walked away, which was a relief. For a second I was worried that, if wishes really do come true, he might have a broken back.

    I took my present upstairs but I didn't open it for ten minutes. The address was in neat capitals.

I traced the letters on the brown paper with my finger, imagining Mum writing my name as nicely as she could. Then all of a sudden I couldn't wait a second longer and I ripped off the wrapping paper and screwed it up into a little ball and chucked it on the floor. Inside was a plain box that didn't give anything away. Rose liked boxes, Dad told me once, and she used them to make spaceships and castles and tunnels. He said she liked the boxes better than the presents when she was a little girl.

I'm not Rose so I was relieved when something rattled against the cardboard when I shook the box. I opened it up. My heart felt like a wild rabbit you see in car headlights in the countryside. At first it sort of froze, too scared to move, but then it exploded and jumped about really fast. Inside the box was some red and blue material. I tipped it onto the bed with one of those grins that hooks on your ears like a hammock on palm trees. The material was soft and the spider sewn on the front was big and black and dangerous. I pulled the Spider-Man t-shirt over my head and looked in the mirror. Jamie Matthews had disappeared. In his place stood a superhero. In his place stood Spider-Man.

If I'd been wearing my new t-shirt in the park, I would not have been scared of those girls. I'd have run after Jas and leapt on a swing, landing on one foot without wobbling. I would have swung higher and faster than anyone ever has before and then I would have jumped off and flown through the air and those girls would have said *Wow*. Then I would have laughed so loud like *HAHAHAHAHA* and probably even sworn or something. I would not have stood ten metres away going all red and shaky like a coward.

On the card there was a football player wearing an Arsenal kit. Mum probably thought it was Man Utd 'cos they both play in red. In the card she had written *To my big boy on his tenth birthday. Have a great day, love from Mum* with three big kisses underneath. I didn't think I could get any happier until I saw the P.S. at the bottom. *I'm looking forward to seeing you in your t-shirt very soon.*

I repeated that sentence over and over and it's still circling my head now, like a dog chasing its tail. I'm sitting on the cushion by the window and Roger is purring. He knows it's been a good day. The stars are shining more brightly than ever before and they look like hundreds of candles on a black birthday cake. Even if I could blow them out, I wouldn't wish for anything else. Today has been perfect.

I wonder if Mum has already booked her train. Or maybe Nigel has a car that he will let her borrow, though I don't think she'd like to drive all the way up here on the motorway. She hates getting stuck in traffic and walks everywhere in London. But she'll get here somehow 'cos she will want to see me before I start school to say *Good luck* and *Be good* and all of that Mum stuff. And she will definitely want to see me in my new t-shirt. I am not going to take it off until she gets here, just in case. I'll sleep in it too 'cos superheroes are never off duty and she might arrive late after a train delay or a traffic jam. It might not be tonight or tomorrow or even the next day, but if Mum said *Very soon* then she meant *Very soon*, and I will be ready for her when she gets here.

4

My teacher made me sit next to the only Muslim in the school. She said *This is Sunya* and stared at me when I didn't sit down. Mrs Farmer's eyes don't have any colour. They are paler than grey. They look like TVs that have lost reception and gone fuzzy. She has got a mole on her chin and two hairs curl out of the middle. It wouldn't be difficult to pluck them out. Maybe she doesn't know they're there. Or maybe she likes them. *Is there a problem* said Mrs Farmer and everyone in my class turned to watch. I wanted to shout *Muslims killed my sister* but it didn't seem like the kind of thing you say before *Hello* or *I'm Jamie* or *I am ten years old*. So I just sat down at the very edge of the table and tried not to look in Sunya's direction.

Dad would go mental if he knew. He thinks the best thing about leaving London is getting away from the Muslims. *None of that foreign stuff in the Lake District* he said. *Just real British people minding their own business*. In Finsbury Park there were thousands of them. The women wore these long cloths over their heads like they were dressed up as ghosts and ready for Halloween. There was a mosque down the road from the flat and we'd see them all going to pray. I really wanted to have a look inside, but Dad told me to keep away.

My new school is tiny. It is surrounded by mountains and trees and a stream runs past the front gate so if you are in the playground you can hear this gurgle gurgle like water running down a plughole. In London my school was on a main road

21

and all you could hear or see or smell was traffic.

After I had got out my pencil case, Mrs Farmer said *Welcome to our school* and everyone clapped. She said *What is your name* and I said *Jamie* and she said *Where have you come from* and someone whispered *Loser land* but I said *London*. Mrs Farmer said she would love to visit London but it was too far to drive and my tummy clenched 'cos Mum suddenly felt miles away. She said *Your records haven't arrived from your old school yet, so why don't you tell us something interesting about yourself*. I couldn't think of a single thing to say. So Mrs Farmer said *How many brothers and sisters have you got* and I couldn't even answer that 'cos I don't know if Rose counts. Everyone started giggling and Mrs Farmer said *Shhh children* and then she asked *Well, do you have any pets*. I said *I have a cat called Roger*. Mrs Farmer smiled and said *Roger the rat sounds very nice indeed*.

First we had to write two pages under the title My Wonderful Summer Holiday and take extra care to put full stops and capital letters in the right place. That was easy enough but trying to think of something wonderful to write was more difficult. Watching Spider-Man and getting my presents from Mum and Jas were the only good things that happened this summer. I wrote them down and they just about filled one page 'cos I made my handwriting really big. Then I sat and stared at my book and wished I could write about ice creams or theme parks or swimming in the sea.

Five minutes left Mrs Farmer said, drinking coffee and checking her watch. *Everyone should be able to fill two pages and some people might even manage three*. A boy looked up. Mrs Farmer winked at him and the boy's face seemed to swell. Then he leaned over so far his nose almost touched the table and he started writing really fast, thousands of words flying out of his pen as he described his wonderful holiday.

Three minutes left Mrs Farmer said. My pen was stuck at the top of page two and it had made an ink splodge 'cos I hadn't moved it for seven minutes.

Make it up. These words were whispered so quietly, I thought I'd imagined them. I looked at Sunya and her eyes were bright and twinkly like puddles in sunshine. They were dark brown, almost black, and she had a white cloth over her head that completely covered every single hair but one. The hair hung near her cheek and was black and straight and shiny like a thin piece of liquorice. She was left-handed and six bracelets jangled on her wrist as she wrote. *Make it up* she said again and then she smiled. Her teeth looked white next to her brown skin.

I didn't know what to do. Muslims killed my sister but I didn't want to get in trouble on my first day of school. I rolled my eyes like I thought Sunya's advice was rubbish but then Mrs Farmer shouted *Two minutes to go*. So I started writing as fast as I could, making up fast rollercoasters and trips to the beach and finding crabs in rock pools. I described Mum laughing her head off when seagulls tried to eat her fish and chips and Dad building me the biggest sandcastle in the entire world. I wrote that it was so big my whole family could fit inside but that sounded made up so I crossed it out. I said Jas got sunburn but Rose got a tan. I paused for about one millisecond when I wrote that last bit 'cos, even though everything else was a lie, that was

23

the biggest one of them all. But then Mrs Farmer shouted *Sixty seconds left* and my pen raced across the page and before I knew it I'd written a whole paragraph about Rose.

Mrs Farmer shouted *Time's up*. She said *Who would like to tell the class about their holiday* and Sunya's hand shot into the air and the bracelets tinkled like those bells you get on shop doors. Mrs Farmer pointed at her and then at the boy with the swollen face and then at two girls and then at me, even though I hadn't put my hand up. I wanted to say *No thank you* but the words got stuck near my tonsils. When I didn't move, she said *Come on James* in this cross way so I got to my feet and walked to the front of the class. My shoes felt heavier than normal and someone pointed at the stain on my Spider-Man top. Coco Pops turn the milk chocolatey, which is good for drinking but makes a mess if you spill it.

The boy read first and it went on and on and Mrs Farmer said *How many pages was that, Daniel* and Daniel said *Three and a half* and his eyes almost popped, his face was so puffed up with pride. Then a girl called Alexandra and a girl called Maisie described their holidays, which were full of parties and new puppies and trips to Paris. Then it was Sunya's turn.

She cleared her throat. Her eyes narrowed to two sparkly slits. *It should have been a wonderful holiday* she said. She paused dramatically and looked around the room. Somewhere outside a truck rumbled by. *The hotel looked lovely on the website. It was in a beautiful forest, with no other houses for miles around. A perfect place for a rest, Mum said. She couldn't have been more wrong.* Daniel rolled

24

his eyes. *On the first night I couldn't sleep because there was a storm. I heard this tap tap tap on my window and I thought it was just a branch, blowing in the wind. But it didn't stop even when the wind died down, so I climbed out of bed and opened the curtains.* Sunya suddenly screamed at the top of her voice and Mrs Farmer almost fell out of her chair. Then Sunya spoke as fast as she could and said *Instead of a branch there was a dead hand knocking on the glass and then a face appeared and it had no teeth and scraggily hair and it said Let me in little girl, let me in. So I—*

Mrs Farmer stood up with her hand on her chest. *Very entertaining as always, Sunya. Thank you very much.* Sunya looked annoyed that she hadn't been allowed to read to the end. Then it was my turn. I got through it as quickly as I could, mumbling all the bits about Rose. I felt guilty for telling everyone she'd been having fun on the beach when really she was inside an urn on a mantelpiece. *How old are your sisters* Mrs Farmer asked. *Fifteen* I replied. *Oh, are they twins* she said, as if that was the best thing in the world. I nodded and she said *How lovely.* My face flushed the exact colour of pink highlighter pen. Sunya stared at me for too long. I knew she was trying to work out which bit of my story was made up, and it got on my nerves so I glared back. Instead of looking embarrassed, she smiled her big white smile and winked like we were sharing a secret.

Excellent Mrs Farmer said. *You are all one step closer to Heaven.* Daniel beamed but I thought this was stupid. Our writing was okay but I don't think it would have impressed Jesus. But then Mrs Farmer leaned over her desk and for the first time I looked at the display. There were fifteen fluffy clouds going diagonally up the wall. In the top right corner was the word HEAVEN in letters cut out from gold cardboard. In the bottom left corner were thirty angels, each with its own pair of huge silvery wings. Written on each angel's right wing was the name of someone in the class. The angels would have looked quite holy if they hadn't got pins stuck through their heads. With a plump hand, Mrs Farmer moved my angel onto the first cloud. Then she did the same with Alexandra's and Maisie's, but she flew Daniel's angel right past cloud one and perched it on cloud two.

At lunchtime I tried to make a friend. I don't want it to be like London here. At my old school, everyone called me *Girly* 'cos I like art, *Geek* 'cos I'm clever, and *Weirdo* 'cos I find it hard to speak to people I don't know. Jas said this morning *It's important to make friends this time*, and the way she said it made me feel uncomfortable, like she knew I spent lunchtimes in the library rather than the playground in London.

I walked around looking for someone to talk to. Sunya was the only person on her own. Everyone else from my class was in a big gang on the grass. The girls were making daisy chains and the boys were kicking a ball about. I wanted to play more than anything in the world but I didn't dare ask if I could join in. Instead, I lay down nearby and pretended to sunbathe and hoped that one of the boys would call me over. I closed my eyes and listened to the stream gurgle and the boys laugh and the girls squeal when the ball got too close.

I thought a cloud must have covered the sun 'cos suddenly I was in the shade. I looked up and all I

26

could see were two glittery eyes and dark brown skin and one hair wafting gently in the breeze. I said *Go away* and Sunya said *Charming* and she plonked herself next to me and grinned. I said *What do you want* and she said *A word with Spider-Man* and then she opened her palm, which was surprisingly pink, and inside was a ring made out of Blu-Tack.

I'm one too she whispered, looking all around to make sure no one was listening. I wanted to ignore her but I was intrigued so I said *You are what exactly* and then I yawned on purpose to make it look like I didn't really care about the answer. *Isn't it obvious* she said, pointing at the cloth wrapped around her head and shoulders. I sat up with a jerk. My mouth must have been hanging open 'cos a fly flew in and landed on my tongue. I coughed and spat and Sunya laughed. *We're the same* she said, and I shouted *We are not*. Daniel looked over from the gang on the grass. *Take it* she smiled, holding out the ring. I shuffled backwards on my knees and shook my head. This was obviously some sort of Muslim tradition, though I'd never heard of the giving and receiving of Blu-Tack rings when we'd studied Ramadan at school. *Go on* she said, wiggling the middle finger on her right hand. A thin line of Blu-Tack was wrapped around it, a little brown stone stuck on top like a diamond. She said *The magic won't work unless you wear one too* and I said *My sister was blown up by a bomb* and scrambled to my feet and ran off.

Luckily a fat dinner lady blew the whistle so I sprinted all the way back to the classroom. When I sat down on my chair, my brain banged against the bones in my head and I needed a drink. My hands made sweat marks on the table. There was laughter

27

in the corridor as the gang from the grass walked in. Every single one of them had a daisy chain wrapped around their wrist. Including the boys. And though they looked stupid, I wished that I had a bracelet of flowers to wear too. Sunya came in last, nothing on her wrist either. She grinned when she saw me and fluttered her fingers in front of my face, the middle one flashing with the Blu-Tack ring.

We did a bit of Maths and finished off with Geography. I didn't look at Sunya once. I felt confused and upset, as if I had betrayed Dad. Even though my skin's white and I have an English accent and I think it's wrong to blow up people's sisters, I must have done something to convince Sunya I wanted Muslim jewellery.

The teacher said *Pack away* and I went to put my Geography book in my new drawer. It says *James Matthews* on the front and there is a picture of a lion next to my name, which made me think of the silver one in the sky. I opened my drawer and saw something small and white underneath my English book. Petals. I glanced up to see Daniel smiling at me. He nodded and pointed, encouraging me to look closer. I moved my English book to one side and my heart leapt out of my chest. A daisy chain. Daniel put his thumbs in the air. My hands trembled as I did it back and all of a sudden I couldn't wait to get home to tell Jas about my day. Sunya appeared at my side, examining the bracelet with a strange look on her face. Jealousy. I picked it up carefully, desperate to wrap it around my wrist, but it fell to bits. Daniel started to laugh. My heart smashed back into my chest making a big black hole that leaked happiness all over the classroom floor. It wasn't a bracelet. It had never been a bracelet—

28

just a bunch of squashed up flowers. And Sunya
wasn't jealous. She was angry. She glared at Daniel
with her bright bright eyes and all the sparkle had
turned as sharp as broken glass.

Daniel tapped a boy called Ryan on the shoulder.
He whispered something in Ryan's ear. They
grinned at me and put their thumbs high into the
air. Then they did one of those sniggers and walked
out of the classroom. I wished the silver lion in
the sky would charge down to Earth and bite their
heads off.

The ring will protect you Sunya whispered and I
jumped a million metres off the floor. We were
the only two left in the classroom. *That is part
of its magic.* I said *I don't need protecting* and
Sunya laughed. *Even Spider-Man needs a bit of
help sometimes.* The sun was pouring through the
window and bouncing off the scarf on Sunya's head,
and for a millisecond I thought about pure things
like angels and halos and Jesus and white icing.
But then a picture of Dad's face filled my mind
and squashed all the other thoughts away. I could
see his thin lips and narrow eyes as he said *Muslims
infect this country like a disease*, which isn't exactly
true. They're not contagious and they don't give you
red spots like chicken pox, and as far as I know they
don't even cause a temperature.

I took a step backwards and then another and
I knocked into a chair 'cos my eyes were stuck on
Sunya's face. As I reached the door, she said *Don't
you understand* and I said *No.* She was silent then
and I was scared the conversation was over. I sighed
like she was the most boring person in the whole
world and I turned my back as if I was about to
leave. Then she said *Well, you should understand*

29

because we are the same. I stopped walking and spoke clearly. *I am not a Muslim*. Sunya's laughter tinkled like the bracelets on her wrist. *No*, she said, *but you are a superhero*. My head snapped back. My eyes grew from marbles to snooker balls. With a brown finger, she pointed at the material draped over her hair and down her back. *Spider-Man, I am Girl M*. Then she walked over to me and touched my hand, and before I could snatch it away she had gone. Mouth dry, eyes as big as planets, I watched Sunya run down the corridor, and for the first time I noticed that the scarf flapping around her body looked exactly like a superhero's cape.

5

It happened five years ago today. The TV's full of it, programme after programme about September 9th. It is Friday so we couldn't go to the seaside 'cos of school. I think we are going tomorrow instead. Dad hasn't said anything but I saw him looking on the Internet at St. Bees, the nearest beach around here, and last night he stroked the urn as if to say goodbye.

He probably won't do it so I am not going to say goodbye just yet. I will say goodbye if he actually lets go of Rose's ashes and sprinkles them in the sea. Two years ago, he made me touch the urn and whisper my last words and I felt stupid 'cos I knew she couldn't hear me. And I felt even more stupid when she appeared back on the mantelpiece the very next day and my goodbye had been pointless.

Jas took the day off school 'cos she was too

upset. I sometimes forget that Rose was her twin and they spent ten years together, or ten years and nine months if you include the bit in the womb. I wonder if they looked at each other when they were in Mum's tummy. I bet Jas had a peep. She's really nosy. The other day I caught her in my room, going through my school bag. *Just checking you've done your homework* she said, which used to be Mum's job.

It must have been squashed, two babies inside Mum. That's probably why they weren't that close. Jas told me that Rose was bossy and always had to be the centre of attention, crying if she didn't get her own way. *I'm glad she died and not you* I said, smiling in a kind way. Jas frowned. *If one of you had to, I mean*. Her bottom lip wobbled. *Isn't it even a little bit nice without her* I asked, feeling cross. Jas had called Rose annoying, not me. *Imagine a shadow without a person* she replied. I thought of Peter Pan. His shadow had much more fun in Wendy's room when Peter wasn't there. I wanted to explain this to Jas but she had started to cry so I gave her a tissue and turned on the TV.

When I was eating my Coco Pops this morning, Jas asked if I wanted to stay off school as well. I shook my head. *You sure* she said, looking at her horoscope on the laptop. *You don't have to go in if you're upset*. I grabbed the sandwiches she had made for my lunch off the sideboard. *We do Art on Friday and it's my favourite* I explained. *And it's year six's turn for the tuck shop*. I sprinted upstairs to get my twenty pounds from Granny.

In Assembly the teacher said a prayer for all the families affected by September 9th and I felt as though there was a spotlight on my head. In

London I hated September 9th 'cos everyone at school knew what had happened. No one talked to me all year but on that day everyone wanted to be my friend. They said *You must miss Rose*, or *I bet you miss Rose*, and I had to say *Yes* and nod sadly. But here no one knows a thing so I don't have to pretend and I want to keep it that way.

When we all said *Amen*, I looked up from the prayer. For a millisecond I thought I'd got away with it, but then I saw two twinkling eyes. Sunya was sitting with her legs crossed, her chin resting on her left hand, and she was biting the tip of her little finger and staring in my direction. I suddenly remembered saying *My sister was blown up by a bomb*, and I could tell from the way that Sunya looked at me, she remembered too.

I haven't spoken to her since I found out she was a superhero. I want to ask all about Girl M but every time I open my mouth I think about Dad and my lips snap shut and trap my words. If he knew I wanted to talk to a Muslim, he would throw me out and I would have nowhere to go 'cos Mum lives with Nigel. It has been two weeks since she sent the present and she hasn't visited yet. The Spider-Man top's getting dirty but I can't take it off 'cos that would be giving up on her. And anyway, it's not Mum's fault she's stuck in London. It's Mr Walker's. He's her boss at the art college and meaner than the meanest person I can think of, which right now is The Green Goblin in Spider-Man. Once he wouldn't let Mum go to a friend's wedding, even though she asked dead nicely. And another time he wouldn't let her have time off for Mrs Best's funeral. Mum said she wasn't bothered about missing the burial 'cos Mrs Best was a batty old busybody, but she'd bought a black dress from Next that she couldn't return 'cos Roger had eaten the receipt.

On one of the documentaries on TV, there was someone talking about losing their niece on September 9th and they couldn't say more than four words without bursting into tears. News reporters phoned Mum and Dad all the time. They never gave any interviews. I wouldn't mind if someone wanted to film me and ask questions, but I don't remember anything about the day except a big bang and lots of crying.

I think Dad blamed Mum and that's why they started to hate each other. They never even talked. I didn't think it was weird until I went to Luke Branston's house when we were friends for four days and his parents held hands and laughed and chatted. Mum and Dad only said practical things like *Pass the salt*, or *Have you fed Roger*, or *Take your bloody shoes off, I've just cleaned the carpet*.

Jas remembers what it used to be like so the silence upset her. It didn't bother me 'cos I never knew any different. One Christmas, we had a big argument about Scrabble and I bashed her over the head with the board and she tried to put the letters down my jumper. Mum and Dad didn't even tell us off. They just sat in the lounge staring in opposite directions when Jas showed them the bump above her nose. *We are invisible* she said later, trying to get the Q out of my collar. I wished it was true. If I could choose a superpower, invisibility would be top of the list, even above flying. *It's like we're dead too* she went on, finding a T down my sleeve.

We were in Trafalgar Square when it happened. It was Mum's idea to go. Dad wanted to have a picnic in the park but Mum wanted to see an exhibition in the city. Dad loves the countryside 'cos he grew up in the Scottish highlands. He only moved to London when he met Mum. *Life's only worth living in the capital* she once said, which made me think of her sitting in a big L for London.

Jas told me the day started off fine and it was sunny but cold and you could see your breath like cigarette smoke. I was throwing bits of bread onto the ground and laughing when the pigeons tried to catch them. Jas and Rose were running through the birds making them twirl into the sky and Mum was laughing but Dad said *Stop that girls*. Mum said *They're not doing any harm* but Jas ran back to Dad 'cos she hated getting in trouble. Rose was not as good. In fact she was quite bad and according to Jas she was naughty at school, but no one seems to remember that now she is all dead and perfect. Jas held Dad's hand as he shouted *Rose, get back here* but Mum just said *Oh, leave her be* and giggled when Rose spun on the spot, throwing her head back. Birds swirled all around her and Mum yelled *Spin faster* and then there was a bang and Rose was blown into bits.

Jas said the world went black 'cos there was so much smoke and her ears went funny 'cos the explosion was so loud. But even though she had a burst eardrum, she could still hear Dad scream *Rose Rose Rose*.

They found out later it was a terrorist attack. Bombs had been planted in fifteen bins all around London and they had been fixed to go off at the same time on September 9th. Three of them didn't work so only twelve bins exploded, but that was enough to kill sixty two people. Rose was the youngest to die. No one knew who had done it until a group of Muslims posted something on the Internet saying that they had done it in the name of Allah, which is the Muslim word for God and rhymes with something I said a lot when I was seven and a half and wanted to be a magician. *Voilà*.

The TV programme made it look like a film. It was a reconstruction of the September 9th bombings. Rose wasn't in it 'cos they didn't have Mum or Dad's permission, but it was interesting to see what happened in the other explosions around the city. One man who died should not have been in London. His train from Euston Station to Manchester Piccadilly had been cancelled due to a signal failure. Rather than wait around for another train, he decided to do a bit of sightseeing in Covent Garden. He was hungry so he bought a sandwich and he put the wrapper in the bin and then he was dead. If the signal hadn't failed, or if he hadn't bought a sandwich, or even if he'd eaten it a couple of seconds slower or a couple of seconds faster, then he might not have been putting the wrapper in the bin at the precise moment the bomb exploded. And that made me realise something. If we hadn't been in Trafalgar Square, or if pigeons didn't exist, or if Rose had been a good girl instead of a naughty one, then she'd still be alive and my family would be happy.

That made me feel strange so I changed channels. There was nothing on but adverts. Jas came in with her shoulders all slouched and said *Dad's asleep now* and she sounded relieved and I felt bad. I hadn't helped her at all. I'd just turned the TV up as loud as it would go so I didn't have to hear the sick splattering the toilet. Jas said *He'll be better tomorrow*. I said *Want to play Guess The Advert*, which is a game I invented where you have to shout out what is being advertised before it says it on the TV. She nodded but then an advert we'd never seen came on so we couldn't play. It showed a big theatre and a man said *Britain's Biggest Talent Show makes your dreams come true. Ring this number to change your life* and I thought how nice it would be to pick up the phone like a grown up and order a different life as if it was a pizza or something. I'd ask for a dad who didn't drink and a mum who hadn't left, but I wouldn't change Jas one little bit.

You can't wear that tomorrow Jas said, nodding at my t-shirt. *We are sprinkling Rose's ashes and Dad wants us to wear black.* I shouted *Coco Pops* 'cos a Kellogg's advert had just come on the TV.

*   *   *

I must have grown since London. All my clothes are too small. I wore black trousers and a black jumper over the top of my Spider-Man t-shirt but you could still see some red and blue around the collar. When Jas saw me, she rolled her eyes, but Dad didn't notice. He just stared at the urn, which he'd put on the table in the kitchen while we had breakfast. It looked like a giant salt pot but I don't think Rose would taste that good on chips.

It took two hours to get to St. Bees and we listened to the same tape we always do on the anniversary. Again and again and again. Play. Stop. Rewind. Play. Stop. Rewind. The tape is going all crackly but you can still hear Mum playing the piano and my sisters singing The Courage To Fly.

Your smile lifts my soul into the sky. Your strength gives me the courage to fly. A kite, I soar so grounded yet free. Your love brings out the best in me. They recorded it for Dad's birthday about three months before Rose died.

Perfect Dad said on Rose's solo bit, sounding choked. *Voice of an angel.* Anyone with ears can hear that Jas is a better singer and I told her so when we were in the car. Wasn't hard. We were squashed up in the back. Rose had the front seat. Dad even put a seatbelt around the urn but forgot to tell me about mine.

We came off the motorway and went down a hill and all of a sudden there was the sea, a line of blue all straight and sparkly as though someone had drawn it with a glitter pen and ruler. The line got thicker and thicker as we got closer and closer and Dad's seatbelt must have been too tight 'cos he started pulling it away from his chest as if it was stopping him from breathing. When we pulled into the car park, Dad tugged at his collar and a button pinged off and hit the exact middle of the steering wheel. I shouted *Bull's eye* but no one laughed. The tap of Dad's fingers on the dashboard sounded like a horse galloping.

I was just wondering if there'd be any donkeys on the beach, when Jas opened the car door. Dad jumped. She walked to the ticket machine and pushed in some coins. By the time the ticket appeared, Dad was standing in the car park, the urn hugged against his chest. *Hurry up* he said and I undid my seat belt and climbed out of the door. St. Bees smelled like fish and chips and my tummy rumbled.

When we walked over the pebbles to the sea, I

saw five good skimmers. Skimmers are flat stones that bounce on water if you throw them in the right way. Jas taught me how to do it once. I wanted to pick up the skimmers and play but I was scared of making Dad mad. He slipped on some seaweed and the urn almost ended up on the beach, which would have been bad. Rose's ashes are as small as sand particles so they would have got all mixed up. I shouldn't really know this but I had a look inside the urn when I was eight. Wasn't that exciting. I'd imagined the ashes to be all multi-coloured, beige ones for skin and white ones for bones. I didn't expect them to look so boring.

It was windy so the waves hit the beach hard and disappeared into froth, like shaken-up Coke. I wanted to take my shoes off and paddle but it didn't seem like the right thing to do. Dad started to say goodbye. He said the same things he said last year, and the year before that. Stuff about never forgetting her. Stuff about setting her free. Out of the corner of my eye, I saw something orange and green swoop through the air. I looked up, squinting into the sun, to see a kite whiz past clouds, turning all the wind into something beautiful.

Say something Jas said and I lowered my head. Dad was staring at me. I didn't know how long he had been waiting for me to speak. I put my hand on the urn and made my face go all serious and said *Goodbye Rose* and *You have been a good sister*, which is a lie, and *I will miss you*, which is an even bigger lie. I couldn't wait to get rid of her.

Dad actually opened the urn. In all the anniversaries that I can remember, we had never got this far before. Jas swallowed hard. I stopped breathing. Everything disappeared except Dad's fingers, Rose's ashes and a perfect diamond shape, darting through the sky. I noticed a deep cut on Dad's middle finger, and I wondered how he'd done it and if it hurt. He tried to push his fingers into the top of the urn but they were too big. He blinked a few times and clenched his jaw. His palm trembled as he held it out. It looked dry, like the hand of an old man. He tilted the urn, then changed his mind. He tilted it a second time, further than before. The top of the urn almost touched his palm. A few grey specks dropped out. He snapped the urn straight back up, breathing hard. I stared at the ashes on his hand, wondering which bit of Rose they were. Skull. Toe. Ribs. They could have been anything. With his thumb, Dad touched them gently, whispering things that I couldn't hear.

Dad's fingers curled around the ashes. His knuckles turned white as he squeezed. He looked up at the sky. He looked down at the beach. He turned his head towards me and then stared at Jas. It seemed as though he wanted someone to shout *DON'T DO IT* but we stayed silent. I thought he was going to open his hand and let the ashes flutter away in the breeze, but he gave the urn to Jas and took a step forward. The sea swirled around his shoes. I felt my cheeks go red. Dad looked mental. Even Jas coughed in an embarrassed way. A wave broke on his shins, drenching his jeans. He took another step forward. Salt water fizzed around his kneecaps. Slowly, he lifted his arm into the air and held out his fist. Somewhere behind us a girl cheered as the kite soared.

Just as Dad opened his fingers, there was a strong gust of wind. It ripped the kite from the sky and blew ashes into Dad's face. As Dad sneezed out Rose, the girl screamed and a man with a strong accent shouted *It's coming down*. Dad's head snapped back to the beach. I followed his gaze and saw a big brown hand trying to control the kite string.

Dad swore loudly, shaking his head. The kite hit the ground and the man laughed. He put his arm around a girl and she giggled too. Dad squelched onto the beach and snatched the urn off Jas. Even though she had replaced the lid, he pressed it down hard, glaring at the man as if the wind had been his fault.

You okay Jas muttered. Tears swelled in Dad's eyes and made me think of those drops you get from the chemist when you have an infection or hay fever or haven't eaten enough carrots.

Do you want me to—I mean, I could do it, if you like. I could scatter the—

But before Jas could finish, Dad turned away. Without a word, he walked back to the car, the urn tucked tightly in his left hand. I quickly picked up a skimmer and threw it into the sea. It bounced five times, which for me is an all-time record.

6

Mrs Farmer sat down on her chair on Monday morning. She read out the announcements. There was one about gardening club and one about recorders and one about the football team. My ears pricked up when she said *The Headmaster's running trials on Wednesday at 3pm. Meet on the school field and bring your football boots*. Then she did the register. Everyone answered *Yes Miss*, but Daniel said *Yes Mrs Farmer*. I was surprised he didn't bow. His angel's on the fifth cloud already. Sunya's angel is on the fourth and most people's are on the third. Mine is the only one still on the first cloud.

What did you do at the weekend Mrs Farmer asked and everyone started shouting at once. I kept quiet. *One at a time* Mrs Farmer said, pointing in my direction. *Jamie first. What fun things did you get up to*. I thought about the sea, and I thought about the ashes, and I thought about the candles that Dad lit around Rose once she was back on the mantelpiece. My weekend was too hard to explain. *Can I go to the toilet* I asked. Mrs Farmer sighed. *School has only just started* she replied, which wasn't a yes or a no so I didn't know what to do. I half got up and then sat down. *Tell me about your weekend* she snapped, as if I was being difficult on purpose.

There was a tinkle of metal and a whoosh of air as Sunya's hand shot towards the ceiling. *Please, Mrs Farmer, can I tell you* she asked. Without waiting for an answer, Sunya said *I met Jamie's sisters*. My jaw almost hit the table. *Oh, the twins* Mrs Farmer smiled, leaning forward in her chair. Sunya nodded. *They are really nice* she said. *Both of them*. Mrs Farmer looked at me with her colourless eyes and said *Remind me of their names*. I cleared my throat. *Jas* I said, and then I hesitated. *And Rose* Sunya added. *We all went to the beach and we had ice creams and chocolate and collected shells and found mermaids and they taught us how to breathe under water*. Mrs Farmer blinked. *How lovely* she said before starting the lesson.

You're a freak Daniel said at playtime and everybody laughed. I was sitting on the field on

41

my own, staring at my shoe as if it was the most interesting thing in the world. *And your girlfriend's a freak too*. Everyone roared again. It sounded like there were hundreds of them and I didn't dare turn around. I untied my lace for something to do. *Weirdo* he shouted. *Finding mermaids and wearing that stinky t-shirt*. I tried to tie a bow but my fingers were shaking. I pressed my teeth into my kneecap and the pain felt good.

I like his t-shirt someone yelled and my heart stopped beating. Sunya sounded breathless, as if she had run from miles away to come to my rescue. The thought made me happy and cross all at the same time. *You are such a sissy* Daniel went on, and everyone said things like *Yeah* and *What a gay boy*. Daniel waited until they were quiet. *Getting a girl to stand up for you rather than face me like a man*. This sounded so stupid I might have laughed if I hadn't been worried about getting my head kicked in. *Men don't wear daisy chains* Sunya shouted and the crowd went *Ooooh*. Daniel couldn't think of a reply. I looked around. Sunya had her hands on her hips and her headscarf was blowing in the wind. Girl M.

Whatever Daniel sighed at last, trying to sound bored, but his face was as pale as his mousey hair and he knew that he had lost. And he knew that I knew and he stared at me with such hatred it made me shiver. *Let's leave these two losers alone*. He walked off, laughing too loudly when Ryan told a joke. And then there was just Sunya and me and it was so quiet I felt like I was inside a TV and someone had pressed the mute button.

I wanted to say *You are brave* and I wanted to say *Thank you*. Most of all I wanted to ask if she still had my Blu-Tack ring, but the words were stuck in my throat like the chicken bone I swallowed when I was six. Sunya didn't seem to mind. She smiled at me and her eyes twinkled and she pointed to the scarf and then she ran off.

*   *   *

For the first time since Mum left, I'm pleased she doesn't live with us any more. The Headmaster's going to phone tonight. He said *Thieves won't be tolerated at Ambleside Primary*. And Mrs Farmer took my angel off cloud one and put it back in the bottom left corner.

It happened after lunchtime. Daniel and Ryan complained that their watches had been stolen. Then Alexandra and Maisie said their earrings had gone too. I didn't think anything of it at first. In London stuff went missing all the time. It wasn't a big deal. But here it was like the number one most serious thing of all time. Everyone gasped. Mrs Farmer jumped up. The hairs on her mole stood to attention like those soldiers in army films.

She made us all empty out our drawers. She made us all turn out our pockets. She made us all tip the contents of our P.E. bags onto the carpet. The missing jewellery fell out of mine. Sunya swore so loudly she got sent out of the room. I got marched off to the Headmaster.

God is watching us all the time Mrs Farmer said as we walked through the library on the way to the Headmaster's office. *Even when we think we are alone, He can see what we are doing.* I thought about being on the toilet and hoped this wasn't true. Mrs Farmer stopped in front of the non-fiction section and turned to look at me. She kept blinking and her breath smelled of coffee. *I am disappointed in you, James Matthews* she said, waggling a fat finger in my face. *Shocked and disappointed. We have welcomed you into our school, into our community, and while this might be the sort of thing that happens in London, it is*—I stamped my foot and the bookshelves shook and Electricity Made Easy fell onto the carpet. *I didn't do it* I shouted. *It wasn't me*. Mrs Farmer pursed her lips. *We'll see about that.*

If I was a thief, I wouldn't be stupid enough to keep the jewellery I'd stolen in my P.E. bag. I'd put it in my pants and take it home instead. I tried to explain this to the Headmaster but it came out wrong and I sounded like a pervert.

Sunya waited for me after school. She was sitting outside the Headmaster's office. She said *Daniel set you up* and I said *I know*. I suddenly felt annoyed. If she hadn't made Daniel cross, he wouldn't have put his watch in my P.E. bag and I wouldn't be in trouble. Sunya tried to say something nice but I shouted *Just leave me alone* and I ran off, even though the sign says *Walk Quietly In The Corridors*.

I sprinted all the way home, scared the Headmaster would phone before I got back to the cottage. My fringe was sticking to my forehead by the time I pushed open the front door. I braced myself the way you do on Bonfire Night and a firework's about to go BANG. But all I could hear was a snore and I was so relieved that my knees gave way.

If Dad's been drinking all day then he'll be asleep all night and I'll get to the phone first. And then I can pretend to be him and he will never know that the Headmaster of my new school thinks

44

that I'm a thief. In a deep voice I will say *My son is trustworthy. Surely you can see that he has been set up*, and the Headmaster will say *I am so sorry*, and I will say *No harm done*, and the Headmaster will say *Is there anything I can do*, and I will say *If you pick James for the football team on Wednesday, we'll forget all about it.*

*   *   *

Jas got home and found me leaning on the kitchen wall by the phone. I tried to make it look natural, like it was just dead comfortable to have the back of my head pressed against the hard wall, but she didn't buy it. *What's going on* she asked and I blurted everything out. She frowned when I told her about Daniel, but she laughed when I said I'd shouted *Men don't wear daisy chains*. It felt nice that she was proud of me, even though it was a lie.

The Head had no idea he was speaking to my fifteen-year-old sister rather than Mum. She sounded so grown up on the phone. She told him that unless he had an eyewitness who saw me put the jewellery in my P.E. bag, it would be unfair to punish me. I could hear the Headmaster stutter. She said that unless he was one hundred percent sure that I hadn't been set up by another member of the class, it would be wrong to put me in detention. The Headmaster didn't even reply. She said *Thank you for informing me of this matter but I am certain that James is innocent* and then the Head said *Thank you for your time, Mrs Matthews* and she said *Goodbye* and hung up. Then we both started to laugh and we couldn't stop and then we had our tea. We had chicken nuggets and microwave chips in front of the TV. Jas didn't eat hers so I got double. She said *You'll never manage all that* but I ignored her. I can eat more than anyone else I know, and at those All-You-Can-Eat pizza places, I can stuff down thirteen slices, or fifteen if you don't include the crusts. Jas said *You're a pig* but I said *Shush*. That advert for Britain's Biggest Talent Show had come on again and it had got me thinking.

7

The engine stopped right outside the cottage and that's when I knew it was Mum in the car. I'd been listening to something rumble down the road but I'd forced myself to stay in bed. I'd run to the window too many times to see Mum turn into milkmen with bottles, or farmers in tractors, or neighbours coming home from work. I couldn't face it happening again. But this time the car didn't zoom past the cottage. This time the car pulled into our drive. Mr Walker must have let Mum have time off at last. I jumped out of bed and straightened my t-shirt and spat on my hand and rubbed it through my hair. Even though Mum hates driving, she'd sped a million miles up the dark motorway 'cos she was so desperate to see me.

I ran to the door and Roger followed me across the room. I was about to turn the handle when I heard a floorboard creak. Jas was tiptoeing across the landing, giggling into her mobile phone. She said *I can't believe you're here*. I waited for her to knock on my door and say *Mum's parked outside*, but she walked straight past my room and disappeared down the stairs.

I followed. Roger kept wrapping himself around my ankles, excited that I was out of bed so late at night. It made it difficult to walk so I picked him up and he purred. I held him against my chest and crept after Jas. I didn't realise I was holding my breath until I reached the bottom of the stairs and my lungs started to ache. Jas was in the porch, a silhouette against the glass. She had her arms wrapped around Mum, whose face was buried in Jas's shoulder.

Granny says that people go green with envy. I don't think that's true. Green is calm. Green is fresh. Green is clean and cool, like mint toothpaste. Envy is red. It burns your veins and sets fire to your tummy.

I shuffled to the letterbox. Roger squirmed so I lowered him to the floor and he ran off down the hall. Jas and Mum started to sway, as if they were doing the last dance at a disco to a song I couldn't hear. Cold air gushed through the gap when I opened the letterbox. I smelled smoke. Nigel's pipe.

I can't believe you're here Jas breathed. *This is such a great surprise*. There was a kissing noise and I imagined Mum putting her lips on Jas's cheek. I squinted through the letterbox but all I could see was a person in a coat. I had to stop myself from sticking out my fingers and clutching the black material. I was scared Mum was going to disappear again. *You can't stay long* Jas giggled. *If Dad finds out I'm dead*. There was another kissing noise. *You have to go* she said. I waited for the *But first say hi to Jamie*. It didn't come. I leaned forward and listened harder, feeling cold all over. Jas was going to keep Mum a secret.

Time to go Jas moaned and I suddenly stood up. Mum couldn't leave without seeing my t-shirt. My blood was one of those marching bands, drumming its way through my heart and my head and that soft place on your neck that goes BOOM BOOM BOOM. Jas was pushed up against the porch door. *Oh baby* she said, which seemed a strange thing to call Mum, but I didn't have time to worry about that 'cos my hand had shot out and was turning the handle.

Jas fell back onto the hall carpet and I opened my mouth to say *Traitor*. But no words came out 'cos this time Mum wasn't a farmer, or a milkman, or a neighbour coming home from work. She was a boy with green spiky hair, a pierced lip and a black leather jacket. I closed my mouth. Then I opened and closed it one more time and the boy said *You look like a fish*. And I replied *Better than a green hedgehog*, which is just about the funniest thing I've ever said. The boy laughed and the *hahas* smelled of smoke. *I'm Leo* he said, holding out his hand like I was important. I shook it and tried to look as if I knew what I was doing. *Jamie* I replied. I didn't know when to let go but he dropped my hand and it swung to my side. I felt very aware of my fingers.

Jas watched all this from the hall carpet. I grinned, happy that she wasn't a traitor. *You sneaky little bastard* she said. Her eyes looked huge when they weren't covered in black make-up. She kept glancing at the stairs, scared Dad would come down, even though we both knew he had passed out in bed.

Leo pulled Jas to her feet. He was tall and strong and perfect. Jas's head came up to his armpit and he wrapped his arm around her shoulder. *Don't tell* she whispered, pushing her body close to his. I felt a bit awkward until Roger brushed against my leg. I picked him up and held him tight.

They started kissing. I watched for about fifteen seconds but then I remembered Granny saying *It is rude to stare*. So I walked off as if it was no big deal to see my sister snogging in the hall at twelve minutes past midnight. The moon lit up the kitchen and there was no colour. It was like being inside Mrs Farmer's eyes. I was angry that she'd accused me of being a thief. I've never stolen anything except grapes from the supermarket when I used to do a big shop with Mum. When she wasn't looking, I'd pick one off the stalk and put it in my mouth and crush it with my tongue so Mum wouldn't see me chewing and guess.

Roger jumped out of my arms. I opened the back door and walked into the garden. The grass felt icy underneath my toes and the air tingled against my skin. Millions of stars twinkled like the jewels in Mum's wedding ring. I bet she doesn't wear it any more. I stared up at the sky and raised my middle finger, just in case God was watching. I don't like being spied on.

Roger's fur glinted in the moonlight and he crawled off, probably to kill a mouse or something. I tried to block out the picture of the furry body he left on the doorstep. I walked to the pond and stared at the water but all I could see was that small grey animal, all cold and stiff and dead. I was glad that Rose had been blown into tiny pieces. I'd hate to think of her under the ground, especially on a cold night like this.

There was a splash. I knelt down and bent over until my nose touched the black water. Somewhere among the floaty plants and swirling weeds, I knew there was a goldfish. Its silky skin is the exact same colour as my hair and I used the same orange pencil to draw us both in my sketchbook. All the times that I've looked in the pond, I've never seen any other creatures. The fish is alone. I know exactly how it feels.

*   *   *

Dad actually got up for breakfast on Tuesday morning. He'd been in bed for sixteen hours and he smelled of sweat and alcohol. He didn't eat anything but he made a pot of tea and I had a cup, even though I don't like it much. Jas yawned four times as she checked her horoscope. *Why are you so tired* Dad asked and Jas shrugged at him but winked at me. I smiled into my Coco Pops and hoped Leo would come again soon.

It was pouring down outside. Jas asked if we could have a lift. Dad agreed and drove us to school in his slippers. I was scared he would see Sunya but all the children were hidden beneath hoods or umbrellas so you couldn't tell who was who. As I jumped out of the car, Jas handed me a waterproof coat and told me to keep dry. She said *You'll catch a cold if you have to sit in a wet t-shirt all day.*

I walked into the classroom and for once I wasn't late. Mrs Farmer wasn't even there yet. Sunya was at our table, drawing a picture. She had ink all over her left hand and on the tip of her nose. I wanted to talk to her but Dad had given me a lift and had said *Have a good day*. It seemed mean to talk to a Muslim when he was trying to be nice.

It started off as a whisper. But then more people

50

joined in, saying it over and over, getting louder and louder, banging their hands on the tables. *Thief. Thief. Thief thief thief.* Daniel was standing in the middle of the group, conducting all the chanters. I looked at Sunya, willing her to come to my rescue. A red felt-tip pen went back and forwards, back and forwards. She didn't even look up.

Mrs Farmer walked into the classroom. Even though the chanting stopped straightaway, she must have heard it down the corridor. I waited for her to tell them off but she just looked at me like I deserved it. She asked for a volunteer to fetch the register and Daniel's hand was first in the air. She smiled at him and his face swelled. Daniel's angel hopped onto cloud six.

At playtime the rain was so bad we had to stay inside. I wasted five minutes sitting on the toilet, three minutes looking at the art displays in the corridor and four minutes pretending to have a headache. The school nurse sent me away with a wet paper towel on my forehead. I was only in the classroom for two minutes before Mrs Farmer came back from the staffroom. Long enough for the chanting to start, too short for it to get really bad.

The windows stopped rattling halfway through History. Rain turned to drizzle. I tried to concentrate on The Victorians but it was hard and I didn't do my best writing like Mrs Farmer said. I described the life of a chimney sweep but I only wrote three sentences 'cos I was worried that if we were sent outside at lunchtime, I would get my head kicked in.

The fat dinner lady with the whistle came into our classroom at the end of the lesson. She said *You're allowed in the playground* and everyone cheered apart from me.

It started as soon as I got outside. They ran at full speed and swarmed around me and I suddenly knew why Granny says circles can be vicious. Every time I tried to push my way out, a pair of hands shoved me back in. They stamped their feet. They clapped their hands. The chant was louder than ever before. I looked around for the dinner lady. She was at the other side of the playground, shouting at some boys for going on the wet grass. I looked around for Sunya and saw a white scarf bounce up the stairs. It disappeared through a door near our classroom. She had gone.

My fingers found my ears. I screwed up my eyes. The t-shirt felt dead big and the sleeves flapped around my arms. I wasn't brave. And I wasn't Spider-Man. I was glad Mum couldn't see me.

Ryan lost interest first. He kicked my shin and said *See you later, loser*. He walked off and everyone followed and ten seconds later only Daniel was left. *Everyone hates you* he said and I stared at the ground. He stamped on my foot and spat in my face, hissing *Get out of our school and go back to London*. I wished I could. I wished I could leave at that very moment and trust that Mum would be pleased to see me. *Go back to London* he said again, as if it was easy. Like I'd be welcome there.

A girl with pigtails tapped Daniel on the shoulder. *Mrs Farmer wants to see you in the classroom* she said, sucking a pink lollipop. *Why* he asked. *Didn't say* was the reply. He shrugged and walked off. I wiped the spit off my face. It was over. I sat on a bench and tried to stop shaking. Daniel asked the fat dinner lady if he could go inside. She nodded. I watched him climb up the stairs and disappear through the door.

After lunch Mrs Farmer made us sit on the carpet. My body ached but I tried not to show it in my face. Sunya sat down last and her eyes were even brighter than usual. Even though I was right at the back, she climbed over the legs of everybody else and plonked herself next to me. She grinned but I didn't know why. Four hairs had come loose from her headscarf and she twisted them around her red, inky fingers.

Some number puzzles appeared on the interactive whiteboard. I stared at Daniel. He didn't seem upset so he couldn't have been in trouble with Mrs Farmer. When Maisie answered a difficult question, Mrs Farmer walked over to the display above her desk. Sunya's fingers stopped moving. She seemed to be holding her breath. *Excellent work, Maisie* said Mrs Farmer, reaching for her angel. *You are one step closer to—* Mrs Farmer gasped. Everyone jumped. Her hand hovered in mid-air. Her mouth hung wide open. Her eyes were glued to something on the wall.

There, stuck in the bottom left corner of the display, were four red letters: HELL. And, in Hell, was a picture of the devil, labelled carefully in neat handwriting. Mrs Farmer.

Who did this she said, her voice no more than a whisper. She couldn't take her eyes off the devil. Neither could I. It was brilliant. It had spiky horns and evil eyes and a long tail. It was bright red apart from a brown circle on its pointy chin that looked suspiciously like a mole.

Nobody spoke as Mrs Farmer hurried out of the room. Less than two minutes later, she was back with the fat dinner lady and the Headmaster

53

all smart in his black suit and shiny shoes and silk tie. *It must have happened at lunchtime* Mrs Farmer said, blowing her nose hard. *Did anyone leave the playground* the Headmaster asked the dinner lady, glancing in my direction. The dinner lady fiddled with her necklace and looked at all of our faces. Sunya's arm trembled slightly. The dinner lady nodded. *He did, Headmaster.* She pointed directly at Daniel.

Come with me, *young man* the Headmaster said, but Daniel didn't move. *Mrs Farmer asked to see me* Daniel protested, going pale. *That's why I came inside.* The Headmaster asked Mrs Farmer if it was true. She shook her head. *Ask him* Daniel exploded, flinging his hand in my direction. *Jamie was there when it happened.* It was only a tiny movement, a nudge of Sunya's elbow, but I understood at once. Daniel's voice was pleading now. He was scared. *Tell them, Jamie. Tell them what that girl with the pigtails said.* For the first time that day, I looked him straight in the eye. *Sorry, Daniel. I don't know what you're talking about.*

Mrs Farmer was too upset to teach us so the fat dinner lady read us some stories instead. When it was time to go home, everyone raced out of the classroom, all except Sunya. I wanted to say something but I didn't know where to begin. So I just opened my pencil case and made sure my pens were all facing the same way. When I had nothing left to do, I looked up to find Sunya watching me, licking a pink lollipop. It was identical to the one the girl had been sucking when she'd told Daniel to go inside. *Bribery* Sunya shrugged, as if her idea had been simple rather than the number one best plan in the entire world and probably the universe, which

Mrs Farmer says goes on and on forever without stopping.

I nodded and my head spun and I felt scared and giddy all at the same time, like you do when you're about to get on a rollercoaster. Sunya reached into her pocket and pulled out two Blu-Tack rings. One of them had a brown stone stuck in the middle. The other had a white stone. Without speaking, she walked over to me, her sparkling eyes like spotlights on my face. Then she pushed the brown ring onto her middle finger and handed me the white one, her face all serious. I paused for about a millisecond, then shoved it on my finger.

8

The leaves in the puddles look like dead goldfish. And all the green has turned brown and purple, as if the hills have got bruises. I like the world this way. Summer's a bit too bright for me. A bit too happy. Flowers dancing and birds singing like nature's having a big party. Autumn's better. Everything's a bit more droopy and you don't feel left out of all the fun.

It's almost the end of October, which is just about my favourite time of year. Of all the festivals like Christmas and Easter, Halloween is my best. I love dressing up and I love getting sweets and I'm quite good at playing tricks. Mum didn't let me buy any tricks when I was little so I had to invent my own. She said *Everyone will give you a treat and no one will ask for a trick*, which was the biggest lie she ever told apart from the one about Dad. On the third anniversary of Rose's death, Dad got drunk and had a go at Mum. Same stuff as always about Trafalgar Square and pigeons and how if she'd been stricter then it might never have happened. Mum was painting in the kitchen but she couldn't see the colours through the tears in her eyes. She'd painted a heart jet black by mistake. I pointed it out and I got a brush and went round the outline in brightest red. *Are you and Dad breaking up* I asked when I had finished. Mum sniffed. *We're already broken* she muttered. I dropped my brush into the sink. *Is that a no* I said, just to be sure, and Mum paused then nodded. So that was the biggest lie, but the one about Halloween was almost as bad 'cos it meant I wasn't prepared and it was embarrassing.

When the scary neighbour with the bulldog said *Trick*, I didn't know what to do. He said *Are you deaf* and I shook my head and he said *Do a trick then*. So I asked him to close his eyes and I just pinched his arm. He said the f-word and the bulldog barked as I ran away. I didn't dare go to any more houses that year in case the same thing happened again. But the year after that I didn't want to miss out on all the sweets so I made up some tricks of my own.

This Halloween's going to be better than ever. Sunya's got more imagination than the most imaginative person I can think of, which right now is Willy Wonka. I still can't get over that trick with the devil. No one ever found out it was her and Daniel was suspended for three days. His angel was taken off the display and put in the recycling box.

I didn't know Muslims celebrated Halloween. I said to Sunya *I thought it was a Christian thing*. And she started to laugh and the thing about Sunya is, once she starts, she just can't stop, and it makes you laugh too. So there we were, sitting on our bench in the playground, laughing our heads off, and I had no idea what was funny. She said *Halloween is a British tradition and it has nothing to do with being a Christian*. I almost said *Why do you celebrate it then* 'cos I always forget that she was born in England.

*　　　*　　　*

We meet again, Spider-Man she said. And I replied *How many people have you saved today, Girl M*. She pretended to count on her fingers. *Nine hundred and thirty-seven* she shrugged. *It's been a quiet day*. We started to giggle. *How about you, Spider-Man*. I scratched my head. *Eight hundred and thirteen* I said. *But I started late and finished early*. We exploded into laughter. We do the same joke every single day and it never ever gets boring.

It felt strange seeing Sunya outside school at the weekend. She was sitting under a conker tree with a white blanket by her side and a plastic bag in her hands. Before I sat down next to her, I peered into the trees. They looked orange and shrivelled, like old men after too long in the sun. Dad had gone out to buy alcohol nowhere near the woods, but I was still nervous.

I almost hadn't come. It is one thing to be friends with a Muslim in school and another to meet up with one at the weekend. Sunya asked me to go trick-or-treating and I said yes without worrying about Dad. All I could think about was how many sweets we would get, and what tricks we could play, and how it'd be so much better than all the other Halloweens in London 'cos this time I wouldn't be

57

on my own. But this morning when I stole some bandages to dress up like a mummy, I felt guilty. We ate our cereal in front of the TV and a lady with the same skin colour as Sunya read out the news. Dad said *Bloody Paki on the BBC* like it was a bad thing. *She might not be from Pakistan* I replied, before I could stop myself. Jas's eyebrows disappeared beneath her pink fringe. Dad switched channel. A cartoon came on. *What did you say*. His voice was calm but his knuckles went white as he squeezed the remote. I coughed. *What did you say, James*. Jas pulled a finger across her lips, telling me to shut up. Even though she wasn't wearing her white make-up, her face had gone pale. *Nothing* I said. Dad nodded. *Thought not* he said and he gave the urn a little nod.

It was a relief when Sunya put the blanket over her head. She'd cut holes for her eyes and a long sausage shape for her mouth and you couldn't see any of her skin through the gaps. *Cool costume* I said and she replied *You too*. Mine was a bit weird as I'd run out of bandages and had to use pink toilet paper instead. I said *I just hope it doesn't rain* and she giggled *Or you'll get flushed away*.

Three hours later, we'd done every single house we could find and had two bulging bags of sweets. We sat under the conker tree to eat our stuff. Everything looked black apart from the sky, which glittered with a million stars. They looked like tiny candles and for a millisecond I wondered if they'd all been lit for me and Sunya and our special Halloween picnic. My sides ached from laughing too much and it had probably been the best day of my life. I wanted to tell Sunya but I was scared she'd think I was soft so I just said *That man* and we collapsed all over again. He'd been the last person to say *Trick* and I'd pulled the water pistol out from behind my back. The man had ducked but of course nothing came out. This was what Sunya called the decoy, which means it distracted him while she did the real trick. She threw a stinkbomb into his house. The man didn't see it 'cos his eyes were closed, waiting for the water. Then Sunya yelled *Got ya* and the man closed the door in our faces but we didn't leave. We tiptoed to his lounge window and watched him sit on his sofa. One minute later, his nose wrinkled. Ten seconds after that, he tipped back his head and sniffed the air. Ten seconds after that, he looked at the bottom of his shoes as if he was worried he'd stepped in dog pooh. Sunya put her hand over my lips 'cos I was laughing too loud and, even though her fingers were freezing, my mouth seemed to burn.

Why do you wear that she asked, her mouth full of sweets. *I'm a mummy* I replied. *They wear bandages but I ran out so I had to—* She shook her head. *Not that* she said, pointing at the toilet paper. *That.* Her fingers touched the Spider-Man t-shirt. *I'm a superhero* I said. *I fight crime.* She sighed and it smelled of cola bottles. Through the holes in the blanket I could see her shiny shiny eyes and they were brighter than all the stars in the sky. *Why do you really wear it* she said. She drew her legs to her chest and rested her chin on her kneecap. She was sucking a lollipop really slowly like she had all the time in the world to hear my story. I tried to speak, but nothing happened.

When we left London, Dad spent about an hour trying to push his wardrobe through the bedroom door. He turned it on its side. He tried it upside down. He tilted it one way and then the other but it just would not fit. Words like Mum and Affair and Dad and Drinking were just like that wardrobe— too big to get out. No matter what I did, I couldn't fit them through the space between my teeth.

The lollipop was almost gone when I said *I just like it, that's all*. To change the subject, I said *Why do you wear that scarf thing on your head* and she said *Hijab* and I said *Who jab* and she said *That's what it's called. A hijab*. I said the word over and over again. I liked the way it sounded. And then I wondered what Dad would say if he could see me sitting underneath a conker tree with a Muslim dressed like a ghost, whispering Muslim words in the darkness. And all of a sudden I knew exactly what he'd say and what's more I could see him say it, with his face all screwed up, his eyes full of tears and the urn trembling in his hand.

I stood up. The sweets were making me sick. I'd only eaten a quarter of my bag but I dropped it onto Sunya's lap. *You have them* I said. *I'm going home*. I walked down the road, tearing the bandages off my face and ripping the toilet paper off my body. Half of me never wanted to see Sunya again, but the bigger half wanted her to run after me and say *What's wrong*. I got to a bend. If I walked five steps further, I'd disappear out of sight. I slowed right down and tried not to look back, but my neck wasn't obeying my brain. Before I could stop it, my head had twisted right round and there was Sunya, hurrying after me.

Are you scared, Spider-Man she said. *Superheroes shouldn't run off like that*. As soon as she was by my side, I started walking faster like I wanted to get away, which I did and didn't all at the same time. *I'm not scared* I said. *I'm late. Dad said I had to be home by eight*. Sunya stuffed my bag back into my hands. *You are the worst liar in the whole world* she said. *Want to trade your cola bottles for my chocolate mice*.

Headlights swung around the corner. I recognised the car. Grabbing Sunya's hand, I tried to pull her somewhere safe. Dad was slowing down. My pulse was speeding up. There were no buildings. No walls. Nowhere to hide. *What's wrong* Sunya asked. I wanted to shout *RUN* but it was too late. Brakes squealed and the window whirred and the car stopped right by my side. Dad leaned out of the window and stared. *Trick or treat* I said, dropping Sunya's hand. I held out my arms like a zombie and made my face all lifeless. *Trick or treat trick or treat trick or treat* I chanted, desperate to distract Dad. Sunya still had the material over her head and, if Dad didn't look too closely, he might not guess a Muslim was hidden underneath the costume.

Who's your friend he said, slurring his words, and Sunya replied before I could make up an English-sounding name. *I'm Sunya* she said. Dad actually smiled. *Nice to meet you* he said and his breath smelled of beer. *Are you a friend of James's from school*. Sunya said *We are in the same class and we sit next to each other and we share sweets and secrets*. Dad looked surprised but pleased. *I hope you get your work done too* he teased and Sunya laughed and said *Of course, Mr Matthews* and I just stared and stared as Dad grinned at a Muslim and offered her a lift home.

We fastened our seatbelts. Mine pressed against my chest, making me hot. If Sunya's parents were outside her house, or if the curtains were open, or if they popped out to say thank you, Dad would see

61

their brown skin and go mental. He swerved in the road and I kept thinking about those drink-driving adverts on TV where everyone ends up dead and I felt bad that I'd let Sunya get in the car when Dad was obviously over the limit. But she just ate sweets and chatted away and I could hear the smile in her voice as if all her words had happy faces. She said she'd lived in the Lake District all her life and her dad was a doctor and her mum was a vet and she had one brother at high school and another brother at Oxford University. *Clever family* Dad said, sounding impressed. *It's the house on the right* Sunya replied and we pulled up outside a big gate. Lights glowed behind curtains but there was no one on the driveway.

Thanks for the lift Sunya said as she hopped out of the car with the plastic bag swinging in her hand. All I could see were her dark dark fingers and I prayed harder than I'd ever prayed in my life that Dad wouldn't notice. But he just smiled and said *Any time, love* and Sunya ran off, the white blanket blowing in the wind.

Dad turned around and drove away from Sunya's house. I looked out of the back window and watched Sunya disappear through the gate. Dad glanced at me through the rear view mirror. *Is she your girlfriend*. I blushed and said *No* and Dad laughed and said *You could do a lot worse, son. Sonya seems like a nice girl*. And all of a sudden I wanted to shout *HER NAME'S SUNYA AND SHE'S A MUSLIM*, just to see what he would say. 'Cos I knew full well that if Dad had seen Sunya covered by a hijab instead of a blanket, he wouldn't have thought she was a nice girl at all.

This morning we did Library Work and I was looking at a book about The Victorians, which said that old fashioned ladies stayed at home to care for their children and didn't have jobs and never left their husbands 'cos divorce was hard to get and too expensive. And I was just thinking how I wished I lived in The Victorian Times when I felt a hand on my back. I was convinced it was Daniel so I shouted *Mrs Farmer*, even though the sign says *SSSH It's A Library*. And she said *What's the matter* and I said *He's digging his fingers into my shoulder blade*. The Headmaster cleared his throat and pushed me into the corridor as Mrs Farmer muttered *You must learn to respect your elders, young man*. The Headmaster stared down at me and I could see up his nostrils and I was just wondering if it was difficult to breathe through all the nose hair when he said *What are you doing tomorrow afternoon*. I said *Nothing* and he said *Well, now you are. There's a space on the football team. Craig Jackson's injured.*

Jas said she wouldn't miss it for anything. She reckons I'll score the winning goal. My horoscope's dead positive this week, and anyway she says my boots are enchanted so they'll make me as good as Wayne Rooney. I asked Dad if he was going to come and he burped. I don't know if that means yes or no.

The football trial was over a month ago. I tried really hard but I hardly got the ball. I played on the left wing and then up front and I didn't do much but I thought I'd done enough. Hundreds of butterflies kept me awake the night before the team was announced. And in the morning every one of those butterflies felt as if they'd had ten energetic babies. The Headmaster said the team would be put up on the notice board outside his office at playtime, which meant I had two whole lessons to get through before I found out. In English we were writing poems called Our Brilliant Family. The only rhyme I could think of was Burn and Urn and, as Mrs Farmer thought Rose was alive, I couldn't even use it. In Maths we were doing fractions and I am normally good at them but the butterflies had spread into my brain making my thoughts all fluttery.

Mrs Farmer said *Put on your coats before you go out to play* and Daniel and Ryan ran into the playground without even checking the list. They knew they'd be on the team 'cos they were the only people in year five to get picked last season. I didn't want to look as though I was looking so I went to the library and got out the first book on the shelf, without seeing what it was. My eyes were fixed on the piece of paper on the notice board. Eleven names were written on it, three subs underneath. As I walked nearer, I whistled the first song that came into my head, which was The Courage To Fly 'cos Dad had been playing it non-stop that weekend on the way to St. Bees.

The letters were squiggles, impossible to read. I took a step closer. The capitals at the start of names became clear. There were two Js. I shuffled forward, my lips still pushed out, even though I'd stopped whistling. I read the seventh name on the list. James.

James. James Mabbot. A year five. I wasn't even

sub.

I ran out into the playground. I kicked open the door and charged down the steps and raced around the corner and crashed into Sunya. My library book flew into the air and then skidded across the gravel. She picked it up and looked at the title. In big black letters it said *The Miracle of Me: A Book about Eggs, Sperm, Birth and Babies*. She started to giggle. I snatched it out of her hands.

That night, I read all about the miracle of me as I sat on the windowsill with Roger curled up by my feet. The book went on and on about how I was special and unique 'cos there was only a one in a million trillion chance that I'd turned out to be me. If that one sperm of Dad's hadn't met that one egg of Mum's right at that one moment in time, then I would have been someone different. That didn't sound like a miracle. That sounded like bad luck.

*   *   *

You won't look stupid Sunya said when she found me outside the changing room, too scared to go in. *You're Spider-Man*. I wanted to say that Spider-Man didn't play sport but she was trying to be nice so I kept my mouth shut. *And you have a magic ring*. I looked at the Blu-Tack wrapped around my middle finger and I touched the white stone. It made me feel a bit better. *You'll be brilliant* Sunya smiled. I took a deep breath and pushed open the door.

Daniel was captain before he got suspended for three days. He looked jealous as the Headmaster discussed tactics with Ryan. Ryan was nodding a lot, his arms folded seriously, a ball at his feet like

65

he'd been born with it attached to his toes. Daniel was sitting down, face furious, right leg jiggling. When he saw me, he shook his head, as if he couldn't believe I'd been allowed in the changing room, never mind the team. I ignored him and pulled my shorts out of my P.E. bag.

In the middle of the floor, there was a pile of shirts and I chose a long-sleeved one to cover my Spider-Man top. The Headmaster told us to make a circle and two boys put their arms around me and I had to bite my lip to keep from smiling. He said *This is the most important game of the season* and everyone was silent. No one was breathing. We all stared at the Headmaster as he spoke. *If we beat Grasmere today then we'll be top of the league* and I looked at the players and my heart ached with how much I wanted to win. He said *Some of our first team players are missing, but we'll just do our best with the subs that we've got* and all of a sudden I found the floor dead interesting. I stared at it as the Headmaster said something else I can't remember.

Mums and dads and grandparents were standing at the side of the pitch. Among all the brown and black and ginger heads was a pink one and a green one and one covered by a yellow hijab. I tried to look like I knew what I was doing and did three lunges and ten star jumps while we waited for the other team to arrive. I ran up and down the left side of the pitch and pretended to dribble, even though I didn't have a ball.

Grasmere arrived at last. The referee said *Captains forward* and Ryan stepped up and Daniel went red with envy. Ryan said *Heads* and the ref said *No, it's tails* so the other team won the kick-off. And then the whistle blew and I was playing my first ever match not as keeper.

The first three times I got the ball I was tackled. The boy marking me looked about thirteen and he even had hair on his top lip and a lump in his throat that should have been called an Adam's melon rather than an apple. He was strong and tough and smelled of deodorant like a man. After five minutes, I had mud all over my legs and my kneecap was killing from where I'd been kicked and my feet were tingling in my tight boots, but I had never felt happier. My defender was big but he was slow and I could run past him quite easily.

I tried harder than I'd ever tried at anything and I kept hoping that Jas and Leo and Sunya thought I was good. I kept wondering if Dad was in the crowd and if he was impressed. Every time I got the ball, a commentator's voice boomed in my head. *A brilliant pass into the box by Jamie Matthews* and *Matthews runs around one defender, then another, and another* and *New signing Matthews has had a great first half*.

After forty five minutes we were one-nil down. Our keeper had let in an own goal. Daniel was saying something about him being a sissy who can't play football to save his life and Ryan was laughing but I didn't join in. I know what it feels like to be the keeper of a losing team. We had slices of orange and they made my hands sticky but they were delicious and then it was time for the second half.

We had loads of chances but couldn't get the ball in the net. Daniel hit the post. Ryan hit the crossbar with a header from my corner. Panic felt like a balloon that kept getting bigger and bigger in my tummy as time ran out. And then a boy called Fraser went down in the box and the ref said *Penalty* and Daniel was going to take it but Ryan said *No, I will.* He got it in the top right corner. He ran over to the fans with his hands above his head and everyone followed. By the time I got there, the celebration had stopped and I had to sprint all the way back to the left side of the pitch before Grasmere kicked off again.

I had no energy left but somehow I kept going. Even though my feet ached, I didn't give up, not even for a second. The Headmaster was pacing up and down the side of the pitch getting his shiny shoes all muddy, and he kept shouting things I couldn't hear. There was too much blood in my head and I had that sound you get when you press a shell to your ear. The ref checked the stopwatch and I knew there was just one minute until the final whistle and all of a sudden I had the ball and I ran past my defender. I was on the edge of the penalty box and I still had the ball and I dribbled forward and I still had the ball and there was only the keeper left. The commentator's voice said *Jamie Matthews has a chance to win the match for his team* and I thought about Mum and Dad and Jas and Sunya and I kicked the ball as hard as I could with my left foot.

Everything happened in slow motion. The keeper jumped. His feet left the ground. His arms stretched. The net swung. The crowd's hands flew into the air. The ball had gone in.

The ball had gone in. I stared at the goal and I didn't blink and I didn't move in case it was all just a dream and I was about to wake up. The shell noise disappeared and I could hear shouts and claps and cheers, and the best thing was they were all for me. For some reason I thought of that book I got out of the library by mistake, and I felt special and unique, not quite like a miracle, but not that far off either. Hundreds of hands dragged me down to the ground. All the players dived on top of me and, even though my face was squashed in the mud and I was getting wet 'cos the ground was soggy, I didn't mind one bit. And I didn't want to be anywhere else in the entire world than right there, hardly able to breathe and crushed on the school pitch by ten screaming players.

Nine screaming players. Daniel hadn't come over to celebrate. I didn't realise until I got to my feet and the ref blew the whistle. Daniel was standing alone in the middle of the pitch and he didn't even look happy that we'd won.

Sunya was chanting my name and she kissed the ring on her finger. I looked all around for Dad and then kissed mine too. She waved and ran off and the balloon in my tummy was bigger than ever but it felt good, like an armband or a lilo or something else that holds you up in water. My shoulders got wider and my chest got bigger and for the first time ever, my Spider-Man top seemed to fit.

All the mums and dads walked over to their boys and for a millisecond I didn't know what to do. I was still smiling but my cheeks suddenly ached and my lips felt cracked and my tongue was too dry. But I kept my smile in place 'cos I didn't want anything, not even the fact that Dad's burp had meant no, to ruin that moment. Jas and Leo were snogging but they broke apart and waved so I sprinted over. Jas went on and on about how I was the hero, even better than Wayne Rooney, and Leo shook my hand again and this time I knew exactly what to do. He said *Not a bad goal for a fish* and I said *Better than a hedgehog could do* and he laughed properly, not in that fake grown-up way, and it glittered silver 'cos of the studs in his tongue and lips.

Other families stared at Jas's pink hair and Leo's green spikes and their black black clothes and white white faces. I stared right back until they turned away, and I felt fierce and brave like I'd even be able to fight The Green Goblin from Spider-Man if he had run onto the pitch at that moment. Jas said *See you at home* and Leo said *Catch you later, squirt* and then I was alone and I opened my eyes as wide as they would go so I could take in every single detail of my best day ever. I saw the mud on my knees, and the nets blowing in the wind, and the defender that I beat walking off with sagging shoulders, all 'cos of me. I smiled secretly at the lion in the sky, and I swear I heard it roar.

The Headmaster said *Well played* and squeezed my shoulder and *Fantastic goal* and rubbed my hair. And just when I thought things couldn't get any better, I walked into the changing rooms and all the boys but Daniel smiled and said *Great strike* and *Brilliant game* and *Didn't know you had such a good left foot*. The keeper even shouted *Jamie Matthews, Man Of The Match* 'cos my goal had made everyone forget his mistake and no one was calling him *Sissy Hands* any more. A few people agreed but Daniel snorted and stormed out of the changing rooms. I thought he was just going home, but when his fist hit my face, I realised I was wrong.

It happened half a mile from school on a quiet road. There was no one else around. Daniel must have waited outside the changing room and then followed me home. I didn't hear him creep up behind me 'cos I was having a conversation with Mum in my head, telling her all about the game and saying *Don't cry. I bet Mr Walker will let you come next time.*

There was a tap on my back and I turned around to see five knuckles. They punched my face and my eyeball smashed against the back of my skull like an egg against a wall. My hands flew up to my head and a foot kicked me in the stomach and I fell to the ground. The foot kicked my leg, then my elbow, then my ribs, and I could taste something metallic that must have been blood.

I turned over to protect my tummy and Daniel thumped me on the back. Then he grabbed my hair and shook and blood splashed all over the pavement. He shouted in my ear *That's for getting me in trouble with the Headmaster.* I tried to reply but my mouth was full of blood and guts and something hard that might have been a tooth. He said *You're a dickhead* and *Everyone hates you* and *One lucky goal won't change a thing.* And I was just lying there taking it all until he said *Go back to London and take the Paki with you.* For some reason that word made me cross so I tried to get to my feet but my body wouldn't work.

Daniel stamped on my fingers before he ran off. I lay on the pavement and watched his trainers disappear around the corner. My bones ached and my head throbbed and I felt tired. I closed my eyes and just concentrated on breathing. Air whistled in and out of my nostrils. I must have fallen asleep. The next thing I knew, the sky had gone dark and the mountains were shadows and the trees were black and spiky against a creamy moon.

I limped home. No blue lights flashed outside the cottage. Mum's car was not in the drive. I had no idea what time it was but I knew it was late and I thought Dad might have been worried enough to make a few phone calls.

I opened the front door and waited for Jas to fly down the stairs or Dad to shout *Where on earth have you been*. The hall was silent. Grey light seeped underneath the lounge door and I walked towards it, my body stinging with each step. Dad was asleep on the sofa, a photo album open on his knees, a picture of Rose glinting in the light from the TV. She was wearing a flowery dress, a cardigan and flat shoes with buckles. I stared at Dad for a long time and, even though my body was battered and my eye had swollen to twice its normal size, I had never felt more invisible. It's not a great superpower, after all.

The TV was muted but that advert came on. Britain's Biggest Talent Show. Lots of children danced in the silence, their faces all happy and shiny and their families clapping along in the audience. And when the phone appeared and the words swirled around saying *Ring this number to change your life*, I grabbed a pen off the mantelpiece and wrote the number on the palm of my sore hand.

10

Turns out I hadn't been asleep on the pavement that long. It goes dark so early now it's hard to tell the time. It was only half past six when I turned off the TV and left Dad in the lounge and came up to my bedroom. As soon as I walked in, Roger leapt off the windowsill and rubbed his fur against my bruises. At least one person was glad to see me. At least one person was happy I'd made it home alive. I had a sudden image of Roger dialling 999 with his paw and reporting me missing through his whiskers. A smile pushed my cheeks up to my eyes and it hurt like you wouldn't believe.

Jas got in at twenty one minutes past ten. The hinges of the front door creaked slowly and I could tell she was trying to sneak in without being heard. I crossed my fingers. There was a stamping noise and then a shout. I pulled the duvet over my head and hummed really hard. Dad sounded like he'd been drinking.

He asked her again and again *Where have you been* and she said *Just out with friends*, which was obviously a lie. But I didn't blame her for keeping quiet about Leo. Dad would not like Jas to have a boyfriend, especially one with green hair. He said *Why didn't you call* and I could hear the words Jas wanted to say. I could see them flash into her brain. But she just said *I'll call next time* and Dad said *There won't be a next time* and Jas said *WHAT* and Dad said *You're grounded.*

This was so stupid I would have laughed but I was trying to keep my face still 'cos it hurt too much to move. Dad hasn't looked after us for months. He hasn't cooked us tea, or asked about our day, or told us off for too long to start now. Jas must have had the same reaction 'cos Dad said *Wipe that daft smile off your face*. And she shouted *You can't ground me* and Dad replied *If you act like a child then I'll treat you like one* and Jas said *I'm more of an adult than you'll ever be*. And Dad said *That's ridiculous* and I whispered to Roger *No it's not*. Roger purred and his whiskers tickled my lips. He was curled up next to me, his body a furry hot water bottle against mine. Then there was this silence full of all the things Jas couldn't say.

When I was friends with Luke Branston for four days, we watched this old horror film called Candyman. It was about a man with a hook who appears if you look in the mirror and say his name five times. And ever since I watched that film I have half wanted to try it, and sometimes when I am brushing my teeth I say *Candyman Candyman Candyman Candyman Candy*— but I never finish it off, just in case.

It's like that with Dad. No one's ever said anything about his drinking. Jas's never said anything to me, and I've never said anything to her, and we've never ever said anything to Dad. It's too scary. I don't know what would happen if we said the word *DRUNK*.

I half wanted her to shout it in his face. Roger got too hot and leapt off the bed. The church clock chimed eleven times and I imagined a little old man pulling the rope in the bell tower underneath the stars. The silence went on. I bit my lip and noticed a gap. Daniel had knocked out my last baby tooth.

Footsteps on the stairs broke the silence. I felt relieved and disappointed, both at the same time. My door opened and Jas came in, dumping her bag on my floor. She sat on my bed and started to cry. Black tears full of make-up made lines down her cheeks. Her back felt bony when I gave her a hug. *I can't do this any more* she whispered, which made me feel sick. That's just what Mum said before she walked out. I grabbed hold of Jas's hand, thinking of the kite on the beach at St. Bees and how it had tugged and twisted, trying to get free. I pushed my fingers in between hers and held on tight. I said *Things will change* and she said *How can they* and I said *Don't worry. I have a plan.*

Before I could tell her about Britain's Biggest Talent Show, she grabbed her bag and opened it up. *Have this* she said, handing me a can. *For your t-shirt. So you don't have to take it off.* Deodorant. I thought of the boy on the pitch who had smelled like a man and I sprayed it all over my body. *Better* I asked. *Much* she replied, with the tiniest smile. *You were really starting to stink.*

*   *   *

When Mrs Farmer walked into the classroom, the first thing she did was fly the footballers' angels onto new clouds. As Daniel's angel had been recycled, she wrote his name on a post-it and stuck it on cloud one. Sunya tried to catch my eye but I ignored her. After what Daniel did, I was scared to make him cross.

My angel jumped up two 'cos I scored the winning goal so now I'm on cloud three. Mrs Farmer said *Stand up boys* and we did and she said *You are all one step closer to Heaven* as everyone clapped. She looked at me funny but then shook her head, deciding not to say anything. My eye is all green and black and puffed up with bruises.

At breakfast when Jas said *What's wrong with your face*, I just said *I got elbowed in the match*. I wanted to tell her about Daniel, but she still looked sad and I thought she had enough to worry about. I wondered if Dad was going to ask about the score but he was frowning at something on the radio. Jas looked up from her laptop. *I don't feel well* she muttered and went back to bed. On the way out of the door, I spotted her horoscope on the computer screen. It said *Prepare for a big surprise*, which must have freaked Jas out.

All the way through Geography, Sunya kept trying to talk to me about the game. She was going on and on about my goal, how it was the best thing she's ever seen, including all the football on TV, and how she knew I'd be brilliant 'cos I was Spider-Man. But I'd never felt less like Spider-Man in my life, with my body aching underneath the t-shirt and the sleeves flapping around my arms. And when she said she thought the Headmaster would make me captain next match, I told her to shut up. She said *What did you say* and I said *You don't know anything about football.* Her eyes changed from circles to slits and her lips made a thin line as if someone had drawn them with a very sharp pencil.

She didn't speak to me all the way through English and in Assembly she didn't clap when the Headmaster announced that I was Man of The Match. It should have been the best moment of my life but I felt like Dominic from my school in London. Dominic's disabled and, whenever he did anything, even wrote his name in big spidery letters, everyone went *Wow* and *Well done* as if he'd written a book or something. When the Headmaster described my goal, that's exactly how I felt, like it wasn't that good for anyone else but it was dead impressive for the weird ginger boy who they all thought was too retarded to play football.

At playtime I walked over to our bench. I didn't expect Sunya to be there. I thought she'd be too angry. But there she was, with her nose in the air and her foot tapping on the ground. Her eyes were as black as the hijab on her head and three shiny hairs blew in the wind. She said *I'm ignoring you,* and I said *So why are you speaking,* and she said *I am just letting you know that I won't be talking for the rest of the day.* So I said *But I'm sorry,* and she said *So you should be,* and I said *I thought you weren't speaking,* and then she hit me on the leg. It shouldn't have hurt as much as it did but I swore loudly and put my hands on my thigh. And then Sunya looked from my leg, to my eye, to the scratches on my hands, and her jaw dropped. She jumped up and said *Come on.* Her headscarf swayed from side to side and her bracelets tinkled as she marched down a slope I hadn't seen before. It led to a green shed below the school.

Where are we I asked as Sunya looked all around and then turned the handle of a hidden door. I followed her inside, blinking a few times as my eyes got used to the dark. The room smelled like cobwebs and mud. *This is the P.E. storeroom* she said as she closed the door and sat on a large ball. *I used to hide in here when everyone called me Curry Germs.* I didn't know what to say to that so I picked up a tennis ball and bounced it on the ground. She reached forward and caught it. *What's wrong, Jamie.* I tried to laugh but it sounded false. She waited until I stopped and then whispered *What happened.*

Hot blood rushed into my face and my bruises throbbed. I wanted to tell her but I felt too ashamed. The fat dinner lady blew the whistle and I turned towards the door. Sunya grabbed my hand. I looked down. My white fingers looked nice in her dark ones. She stood up. She was so close I could see a tiny freckle just above her lip that I'd never noticed before. She dropped my hand and put her fingers on the right sleeve of my t-shirt. I shouted *DON'T* but she lifted it up, peeling it back slowly and gently like she knew that my arm was sore. And when she saw the bruise above my elbow, her sparkly eyes shone with tears. *Daniel* she asked, and I nodded.

The whistle blew again so we couldn't talk. We crept out of the door and crawled up the slope and joined the rest of the children without being seen. Through History and Science, Sunya stared at Daniel and I was scared she would say something and make it worse. But she seemed to know how I felt 'cos she kept her mouth shut and when it was lunchtime we went back to the storeroom.

I like it in there. It's quiet and cool and secret. We sat on a mat and shared sandwiches and I told her about the fight. She bit her lip and shook her head and swore at all the worst bits. She said *Let's get revenge* but I said *Just forget it* and she said *But he called you a dickhead. He beat you up. We have to do something.* I was worried she meant tell a teacher but then she said *My brothers will smash his face in.* She knows like I know that teachers make things worse. I thought about Daniel getting kicked by a big boy and it made me feel good and bad all at the same time. I wanted him to get beaten up but I wanted to be brave enough to do it myself.

It went quiet for a bit and I ate the crusts of my bread as Sunya looked at my Spider-Man top. She touched it with her hand and her face was all thoughtful and I knew what she was about to ask. And this time the words like Mum and Affair and Dad and Drinking didn't seem too big to get out.

I told her almost everything. She didn't interrupt. Just listened and nodded. I talked about Dad's bottles in the bin and Mum walking out to live with Nigel. I told her how I thought Mum had forgotten

78

my birthday and how relieved I was to get the present two days later. In the dust on the floor of the storeroom, I wrote the words Mum put in the P.S. of my card, and Sunya agreed that she would visit soon. And when I explained why I couldn't take my t-shirt off until Mum had come to see me, she understood.

All the time I'd been talking, I'd been staring at the golden square of light around the secret door. But when Sunya said those words I looked at her face. She smiled and I smiled and our hands pressed together and a firework whizzed up my arm. It started to rain but the tap on the roof was not as loud as the BOOM of my heart. I wanted to look at Sunya's freckle so I leaned forward and stared at the brown dot above her lip. *It's a superstition* she said and her voice was a bit higher than normal. I leaned even closer. Her breath tickled my face. *A superstition* she whispered. *That's what you've got.* My nose almost touched her three shiny hairs as I said *Super what* and she said *Like those footballers that score goals and have to wear the same sweaty underpants every match for good luck.* And then we started to giggle and the freckle disappeared as her lips stretched into a smile.

All of a sudden our faces felt too close so I stood up and looked around for a ball. I found one in the corner of the storeroom and kicked it about a bit. Sunya said *Tell me about your sister* and I whacked the ball too hard and it crashed against the secret door. I said *She's got pink hair* and Sunya said *I meant the other one.*

Sunya is a Muslim and Muslims killed my sister. I didn't know what to say. I thought about lying but it didn't seem right and I wished Rose had just

79

drowned or burned to death as that would have been so much easier to explain. And then I started to laugh 'cos that was a strange thing to wish and Sunya joined in and then we just couldn't stop.

And through all the laughter I managed to say those four words. *Muslims killed my sister.* And Sunya didn't look shocked, or say *I'm so sorry*, or try to look sad like everyone else who'd found out. She said *It's not funny, oh it's not funny* but then laughed even harder, holding her sides, tears rolling down her dark cheeks. And I laughed too and my eyes were wet for the first time in five years. And I wondered if this was what the counsellor had meant when she said *It will hit you one day and then you will cry.* Somehow I don't think she meant tears of laughter.

11

I like the taste of envelopes and I licked the shiny bit five times before I stuck the top down. I imagined Mum opening the letter in Nigel's house, her fingers touching my dried spit, and that made me feel nice. Mrs Farmer told us it was Very Important for Mum and Dad to come to Parents' Evening in December. She said *This is their last chance to talk to me before you go to High School next year. You should come with your mums and drag your dads along too.*

I got two letters off the pile in the classroom and gave one to Dad and sent one to Mum. I put a note on the top of her letter in my best joined-up handwriting. *Meet outside my new school, Ambleside*

Church of England Primary, on December 13th at 3.15 pm. P.S. Don't bring Nigel. I was going to write *I will be wearing my Spider-Man t-shirt* but I decided not to. I want it to be a surprise. I carefully folded the pages I'd torn from my sketchbook and put them in the envelope as well. A picture of me and a picture of the goldfish. Mum'll love them.

When the letter fell into the post box, I felt excited. Parents' Evening is still two weeks away so there is plenty of time for Mum to ask Mr Walker for time off. She won't want to miss it. Mum always goes on and on about how school is important and good grades can get me anything that I want. She said *Put in the hard work now and you will get the rewards later in life.* I'm going to try really hard at school until December 13th so Mrs Farmer has loads of good things to say.

After I sent the letter, I sat on the wall by the post box and waited for Sunya. I felt bad leaving Dad 'cos he asked me what I wanted to do this morning. He said *Got any plans* and I almost choked on my Coco Pops. I coughed *Off to my friend's* and he said *Oh* in this disappointed way that made me feel like I was doing something wrong. Which of course I was 'cos I was going to have lunch with a Muslim, but Dad didn't know that. He said *I thought we could go fishing* and Jas took a huge gulp of tea and burned her tongue. I said *Sorry* and he said *Well, be back by five because I'm making tea.* Jas was fanning her tongue with her hand but her eyes still widened in shock.

Dad's been much better since that argument with Jas. I think he realised he hadn't been looking after us that much. He still drinks, but not in the mornings, and he has taken us to school four times

81

this month. And he's started asking me about lessons and stuff. Even though he doesn't always listen to the answer, I enjoy telling him. When I said I had scored the winning goal in the football match and my team were top of the league, he said *You should have told me you were playing. I would have come to watch*, which was annoying and nice all mixed together. Jas was painting her nails when he said this and she just shook her head and winked at me and blew on her black fingernails to make them dry.

It's good Dad has changed 'cos Jas thought my plan was rubbish. I told her about ringing Britain's Biggest Talent Show and leaving our address so the TV people could send us information about the auditions. She said *But you need a talent to enter a Talent Show* and I said *You can sing* and she said *Not like Rose* and that made me cross 'cos it's just not true. When the information arrived, I went to show Jas. I pointed at the date, January 5th, and the place of the nearest audition, Manchester Palace Theatre. She said *Not that again* and I said *But it might change our lives* and she said *Stop talking crap* and *Get out of my room.*

I saw Sunya before she saw me. She was running down the hill towards the post office. Her hijab flew out behind her and she really did look like a superhero, zooming through the air. In Maths last Friday, when I asked Sunya if she ever takes the hijab off, she snorted with laughter. *I only wear it outside the house or if people come round.* I said *Why do you have to cover up* and she said *Because it says so in The Koran.* And I said *What's The Koran* and she said *It's sort of like The Bible.* And that is the thing about Christians and Muslims—they both have a God and they both have a book. They are just called different names.

Sunya sprinted to the post box and grabbed my arm and pulled me back up the hill, talking all the time. I felt dead nervous. I'd never been inside a Muslim's house before. I was worried that it would smell of curry like Dad said in London. I was scared that her family would be praying and talking in a different language. And I was frightened that Sunya's dad would be making bombs in his bedroom. That's what Dad said all Muslims do. And though I'd be surprised if Sunya's dad was a terrorist, Dad told me that you never can tell and even the most innocent-looking people have explosives in their turbans.

When we walked through the door, a dog came bouncing up to Sunya. It was black and white with long ears and a wet nose and a tiny tail that wagged madly. Sammy the dog looked like an English pet and not a Muslim one. I sighed with relief. He was normal. And so was everything else. Sunya's house was no different to mine. In the lounge there was a cream sofa and a nice rug and a mantelpiece that had all the right things on it—photos and candles and vases full of flowers not sisters. The only Muslim thing in the whole room was a picture of fancy buildings with domes and spires. Sunya said it was a holy place called Mecca and I laughed 'cos that was the name of the Bingo place down the road from our flat in Finsbury Park.

The kitchen was the most interesting. I'd expected it to smell of spice and have lots of big bowls full of exotic vegetables. But it was just like my kitchen except nicer 'cos there was a packet of Coco Pops on a shelf but no alcohol bottles and the bin just smelled of rubbish.

Sunya's mum made chocolate milkshake and put a curly straw in my glass. She wore a blue headscarf and had Sunya's sparkly eyes but her skin was lighter and her face was slower. More serious. Sunya's face is fast. It changes ten times a minute. Her eyes grow and shrink and her freckle jumps about and her eyebrows wiggle when she talks. Sunya's mum is calm and kind and clever. She's got a strong accent, not like Sunya, and my name sounds different when she says it. She doesn't seem like the type of woman who would marry a bomber, but you never know.

We drank our milkshakes in Sunya's room. We were thirsty 'cos we'd been jumping off the bed and seeing who could stay in the air the longest. 'Cos I am Spider-Man, I had to touch the ceiling and try to stick there for as long as possible. And 'cos Sunya is Girl M, she had to flap her hijab and try to hover above the carpet. In the end it was a draw.

A whole clump of hair had come free from Sunya's pink headscarf, the most I had ever seen. It was thick and glossy and nicer than all the hair in those shampoo adverts where the women toss their heads from side to side. And I said it was so sad that The Koran made her cover up her hair like it was a bad thing. Sunya slurped the last bit of chocolate milkshake and said *I don't cover up my hair because it is bad. I cover it up because it is good.* This was confusing so I kept quiet and blew a chocolate bubble. Sunya put down her glass and said *Mum saves her hair for Dad. No other man can see it. It makes it more special* and I asked *Like a present* and she said *Yeah.* I thought how much better it would have been if Mum had saved her hair for Dad rather than showing it to Nigel, and I said *I understand*.

Sunya smiled and I smiled and I was just wondering what our hands would do when her mum came into the bedroom with some sandwiches. There were cheese ones and turkey ones and they were cut into triangles, but I couldn't eat them. I've always hated that game Pass The Parcel 'cos the music never stops on me so I never get to open anything. And Sunya's hijab looked exactly like pink wrapping paper and I imagined her disappearing, bright and sparkly and perfect, before I could sneak a look under the outer layer.

Sunya had her mouth full of bread so I couldn't tell what she was saying at first. But then she swallowed and said *Do you miss Rose* and it was the first time we'd talked about her since the storeroom nine days ago. I nodded my head and opened my mouth and I was about to say *Yes* like a robot. But then I realised I had never been asked that question before. It's always *You must miss Rose*, or *I bet you miss Rose*, but never *DO you miss Rose*, like there's a choice. So I stopped my head nodding and I changed the word in my throat and I said *No*. Then I smiled 'cos nothing bad had happened and the world hadn't fallen to bits and Sunya didn't even look shocked. I repeated it. Louder this time. *No*. And then, feeling braver, I looked all around and said something else. *I don't miss Rose one bit*.

Sunya said *I don't miss my rabbit either* and I said *When did it die* and Sunya said *Patch got eaten by a fox two years ago*. And I said *How old is Sammy* and she said *Two. Dad bought him when Patch died because he knew I'd be upset*. And that didn't sound like the kind of thing a terrorist would do, and when I walked past her parents' bedroom on the way to

85

the loo, there weren't any signs of bombs either.

After lunch we climbed trees and sat on branches that shook in the wind. Leaves swirled around the garden and clouds raced across the sky and everything felt fresh and free like the Earth was really just a big dog sticking its head out of a speeding car's window. I asked Sunya if her dad was English and she said *He was born in Bangladesh* and I said *Where's that* and she said *Near India.* I can't imagine a place like that. The furthest I've been is Costa del Sol in Spain, which is hotter than England but not that different. There are cafes that serve Full English Breakfasts and I had sausages and ketchup every single morning for two weeks. So I asked *What's it like* and she said *No idea but my dad prefers it here* and I said *Why did he move* and she said *My grandpa came in 1974 to find a job in London.* This seemed like a long way to go to look for work. *Couldn't he have gone to the job centre in Bangladesh* I asked and Sunya just laughed. I suddenly wanted to know everything about her. All these questions charged from my brain to my mouth and the first one to get out was *How did your family end up in the Lake District.* Sunya's legs swung back and forwards under the branch as she spoke. *My grandpa made my dad work hard and stay out of trouble and go to medical school as far away from London as possible. He went to Lancaster and met my mum and they got married and moved here. It was love at first sight* she added, turning to look at me, her legs suddenly still. All the questions I wanted to ask evaporated from my brain like that steam we learned about in Science. *Love at first sight* I repeated and Sunya nodded, then smiled, before jumping right out of the tree.

I made sure I was home by five. When I walked into the cottage, Roger ran out as though he'd been waiting for someone to open the front door. The hall was full of thick smoke. *I hope you like it crispy* Dad said when I walked into the kitchen. He'd set the table and had lit a candle and Jas was already sitting there with her hair all flicked out and fancy, a huge smile on her face. I couldn't believe it. Dad had made a roast dinner and it didn't matter one bit that the chicken was black on top.

The roast potatoes were too greasy and the gravy was too salty and the vegetables were too soggy but I ate every last bit to make up for the fact Jas didn't touch hers. I would have eaten the Yorkshire puddings as well if they hadn't been stuck to the baking tray. We were having a great time and actually talking for once when Dad started to say stuff about Sunya. *Did you know Jamie's got a girlfriend* he asked. Jas gasped as my stomach dropped. *You haven't* she squealed and I went red. *It's the deodorant* she laughed. *That's what it is.* Dad winked at Jas. *She's called Sonya and seems really nice. Young love* he teased, and I said *Daaaaad* in this groany-proud sort of way that didn't ask him to stop.

Jas cleared her throat. I knew what was coming and I gnawed at a chicken leg like Sammy the dog. She said *While we're on the subject, there's something I should tell you.* Dad dropped his fork. *I've got a boyfriend.*

Dad stared down at the table. Jas cut a carrot into tiny pieces. I dipped my fingers in the gravy on

87

my plate. I was just sucking them clean when Dad said *Okay* without looking up. And Jas squeaked *Okay*, and Dad sighed *Okay*, and I felt left out so I said it too. But no one heard 'cos Jas had jumped up and she'd wrapped her arms around Dad and was giving him the first hug I had ever seen. And Jas's face was flushed and happy, but Dad's was tight with a sadness I didn't understand.

Jas sang as she washed up. I stopped drying the plates and looked right at her. *You really have got a good voice*. She replied *I'm not entering that crap contest* and I said *I know* and she said *So tell me about this girlfriend of yours*. I thought about Sunya's freckle and her shiny hair and sparkling eyes and laughing lips and brown fingers and I said *She is beautiful* before I could stop myself. Jas pretended to be sick into the washing up bowl so I whipped her with the towel and then we were laughing. Dad came into the kitchen to put the pots away and tell us off for being silly. We were like a proper family and for once I didn't miss Mum. The silver lion stared at us through the cottage window. It may just have been Roger, but I thought I heard a purr.

12

There were thousands of stars above the cottage, no clouds and the moon was fat. It looked like a saucer of milk and I showed it to Roger. He'd followed me outside and was sitting on my lap, staring at the sky with his clever green eyes. Neither of us could sleep and I was glad he was there to keep me company. My fingers were keeping warm in his fur and I could feel his heart beating against my knees. The night smelled cold and secret like the storeroom and I wondered if Sunya was asleep underneath the blue duvet I'd seen in her bedroom two days ago. And then I felt guilty for thinking about her so I shook my head and blinked three times and stared into the pond, remembering the rules on the rock that God threw at this weird man called Moses.

Today Mrs Farmer said that if we wanted to go to Heaven, we all had to follow The Ten Commandments. She said *God gave them to Moses on a stone up a hill and they are the rules that we should all live by*. At first I wasn't really listening 'cos to be honest Heaven doesn't sound that great. As far as I can tell it is just full of angels singing carols and everything is a bit too bright so I am going to make sure that I am buried with some sunglasses. But then Mrs Farmer said *Number five is one of the most important: respect your mother and father*, and all of a sudden I felt bad. Having triangle sandwiches with a Muslim is not respecting Dad one little bit.

There was a tinkle of bracelets as Sunya's hand shot into the air. *What happens if you break the rules* she said, before Mrs Farmer had asked her to speak. *Don't interrupt* the teacher said. *Do you go to Hell* Sunya continued, her eyes wide. *And is the devil there*. Mrs Farmer went pale and folded her arms. She glanced at the clouds on the notice board and then at Daniel. He stared at Sunya as if he couldn't believe she was bringing it all up again. She ignored him and scratched her temple. *What does the devil look like* she asked sweetly and the class started to laugh. Sunya didn't even smile. She kept her eyes all huge and curious. Daniel's mouth was a big black O in his bright red face. *That's quite enough* Mrs Farmer said, and the words sounded strange 'cos they were being pushed through the tiny gaps in her clenched teeth and made me think of cheese being grated. *Let's look at the other commandments.*

Sunya winked at me and I did it back but rule five made me feel guilty. *Respect your mother and father.* That's what God said. And there I was winking at a Muslim, like it was okay to do something Dad would hate. I suddenly realised that it didn't matter if my angel jumped up every single cloud and got to the top of the display in the classroom. If there was a real Heaven rather than one cut out of gold cardboard, I wouldn't get in 'cos I was breaking a commandment. And for some reason that made me think of Rose. I don't know where her spirit is, but if it is in Heaven, I bet it's really lonely. I imagined Rose's ghost all alone on a white cloud, no elbow, no collarbone, no family or friends. I couldn't get the picture out of my head and it gave me a sickness that lasted all day and stopped me from sleeping.

The bush rustled and Roger jumped off my lap and crept into the night, his belly brushing the long grass. I leaned over the pond and tried to find my fish in the silvery water. He was hidden underneath a lily pad and all on his own so I gave him a stroke. He swam up to my fingers and nibbled them as though they were food. I wondered where his parents had gone. Maybe he had left them in a river or the sea. Or maybe the pond was some sort of Fish Heaven and the rest of his family weren't dead yet. And even though I knew that was impossible, I felt so sad for my lonely old fish that I kept him company for ages and probably would have stayed there all night if the rabbit hadn't started squealing.

I put my hands over my ears and shut my eyes as tight as they would go but the squeal was difficult to block out. The next thing I knew, Roger was at my side rubbing his head against my elbow, a dead rabbit tossed at my knees. I didn't want to look but I couldn't stop my eyes, like when someone's got food or a birthmark on their face and you keep staring at it by accident. The rabbit was only a baby. Its body was tiny and its fur was all fluffy and its ears looked brand new. I tried to touch its nose but every time my finger got near the whiskers, my body jerked away as if I'd been electrocuted. I didn't want to leave the rabbit there but I couldn't bring myself to touch it so in the end I found two twigs and used them like chopsticks. I grabbed the rabbit by one of its ears and carried it away from the pond and dropped it by the bush. I covered the rabbit with grass, leaves, anything I could find. Roger purred at my side as if he'd done me a favour.

I crouched down and looked him in the eye and told him about commandment six. *Thou shalt not murder.* Roger purred even harder, his tail stuck up proudly. He just didn't get it and I felt angry with my cat. I let him back in the cottage but I shut my bedroom door in his face and then I tried to sleep. For the first time ever, I dreamed about Rose.

*　　　*　　　*

Mrs Farmer has stuck The Ten Commandments on the wall opposite my chair. Even if I wanted to forget all about rule five, it would be impossible. It's like Dad's eyeballs are pinned on the display, watching me.

91

At the start of Maths, Sunya kept whispering *What's wrong* and I kept saying *Nothing* but I couldn't look at her without thinking of Rose. Eventually she said *Fine then* and asked me if I had any more ideas for revenge. Sunya's brothers don't think it's right to beat up a ten year old so we need a new plan. She's desperate to defeat Daniel but I don't want to do it. She keeps saying *If you let him get away with it then he will just do it again* but I don't think that's true. Daniel likes to win and now he has won he's lost interest. He hasn't bullied me for ages. He hasn't kicked me or punched me or called me *Dickhead* for days. It's over and I lost and that's okay.

Well, it's not okay but I can't win so I am being a good loser. In Wimbledon there is this tennis player who gets to the final a lot but never gets the trophy. Everyone always says things like *He is a gentleman* and *Excellent sportsmanship* 'cos he just smiles and shrugs and accepts that he is second best. So I am doing that 'cos if I tried to beat Daniel then I'd lose and get my head kicked in.

Halfway through Maths, Mrs Farmer said she had something Very Important to say. The hairs on her mole started to shake and her chin was all trembly. She said *Ofsted are coming* and glanced at the door as if they were about to charge in. Ofsted sounded like an army or something, and I was just wondering if they'd have guns when Mrs Farmer said *They are Inspectors*. Daniel's hand shot into the air and he said *My dad's a Chief Inspector in the police*. Mrs Farmer said *That's enough boasting* and Sunya laughed out loud on purpose. Mrs Farmer said *These Inspectors are not from the police. They are special men and women who examine* schools and give them a grade—*Outstanding, Good, Satisfactory or Poor.* Her face was getting whiter and even her colourless eyes seemed to fade. *Next week they'll watch me teach and it is Very Important to show the Inspectors how well we all work. It is Very Important to behave like good boys and girls. They might ask you questions and it is Very Important to be polite and clever and to say nice things about our class.* Sunya grinned. I knew exactly what she was thinking. I wanted to smile back but I didn't.

At playtime I spent twelve minutes in the toilets respecting Dad. I put my hands under the dryer, pretending it was a fire-breathing monster. My hands were getting burned and the flames were so hot but I was tough enough to take it and I didn't even scream. It was a good game but not as good as sitting on the bench or going through the secret door with Sunya. But I can't do that any more. Just in case there is a Heaven and Rose's spirit is stuck up there alone, God has to let me in too. So I need to follow The Ten Commandments. All of them. Including number five.

*   *   *

It's been two days since I spoke to Sunya. Dad has taken us to school and made tea every day since the roast so I think I am doing the right thing. It is hard though and my tummy twisted when I found the Blu-Tack ring in my drawer. It should be easier now we are not friends, but it was better when she kept asking me *What's wrong* and *Why are you being weird.* At least I could hear her voice, then.

I feel like one of those drug addicts in films that do nothing but think about tablets and the less they have them the more they want them until they go crazy and rob a supermarket to get the money. I'm not saying I will rob the school tuck shop or anything. I don't think Sunya would be my friend even if I gave her all the chocolate in the receptionist's cupboard, which is where the tuck shop is held on Wednesday and Friday playtimes.

Leo came over for tea tonight. Dad made pizza. They were ones from the shop but he chopped up bits of ham and poured a tin of pineapple over the top to make them tropical. Mum used to do that. At the table there wasn't much conversation. Dad was ignoring Leo and Leo looked nervous and I could tell Jas felt awkward too. She kept asking questions she's asked me before. She said *So how's football going,* even though I told her last week that there weren't any matches until after Christmas. And then she said *What's your Headmaster like,* but she knows better than me 'cos she talked to him on the phone. I answered everything as well as I could though. She was just desperate for some noise other than knives scraping on plates and Dad sighing at Leo's green hair.

After tea, Leo kept saying *Thank you* and *That was great, really great* like we'd had a feast instead of supermarket pizzas. And Dad grunted something I couldn't hear and it made me cross 'cos Granny says *Manners cost nothing.* Jas took Leo by the hand and Dad's eyes popped out of his head when she pulled him towards the stairs. He said *I don't think so* and pointed to the lounge. Jas's face was like one of those cooked tomatoes you get in Full English Breakfasts in Spain. I felt sorry for her but I was being respectful so I didn't say a word and just helped Dad do the dishes. He washed everything

94

too hard and bubbles slopped over the sink. I wanted to ask why he was cross but I didn't dare. So instead I told him about Moses and the stone, but he walked off before I'd finished and went to get a beer.

13

Last night I dreamed about Sunya. I kept asking to see her hair and I tried to touch the hijab but she ducked out of the way and pulled it around her head. I asked again. And again. Begging and begging and more and more desperate, but every time I asked, the hijab got tighter and her face got smaller until it covered everything except one of her eyes. Her eye didn't sparkle but just stared and stared and then turned into a mouth that said *Go back to London*. When I woke up, my body was sweaty and my hair was sticky and I missed Sunya so much my heart ached.

In the car on the way to school, Dad was saying *No* and Jas was sulking. She kept saying *But you said Okay* and Dad said *To having a boyfriend, not to going on dates*. She said *We just want to go to the cinema* and he said *Leo's got green hair*. And Jas said *So what* and Dad said *It's strange* and Jas replied *It's not* and I agreed but kept my mouth shut. Dad said *Boys who dye their hair are a bit*—and then he paused. Jas glared. *Are a bit WHAT exactly* she shouted and I prayed to God to throw down another rock to knock Dad out and shut him up. He said *They're a bit girly* and she said *You mean GAY* and Dad replied *You said it, not me*.

Then there was silence and it went on and on until Jas said *Stop the car*. And Dad said *Don't be ridiculous* and Jas screamed *Stop the EFFING car*. Dad pulled up and someone beeped. Jas jumped out. She slammed the door and she was crying and Dad was shouting and the windows were getting all steamy. Someone beeped again. Dad looked in his rear view mirror and said *Don't tell me what to do in my own country*. I wiped the glass and looked behind to see Sunya in the car with her mum. Dad drove off too fast leaving Jas in the rain and he was going on and on about Pakis, about how they don't work and just sit at home all day taking money off the Government before blowing up the country that's keeping them alive.

And all of a sudden as we swerved around a sheep eating grass by the road, the ninth commandment boomed in my brain. *You must not give false evidence against your neighbour*. Yesterday when Mrs Farmer asked what this meant, Daniel put up his hand and said *Don't tell lies about your neighbours*.

I sat up in my seat. *Don't tell lies*. My heart beat a lot faster. *About your neighbours*. The radio came on and the music was loud but all I could hear were the lies that Dad told. *All Muslims are murderers. Too lazy to learn English. Make bombs in their bedroom.* My heart suddenly stopped. Dad's been giving False Evidence. And Sunya only lives two miles away. So he broke the commandment 'cos it says *Don't tell lies about your neighbours* not *Don't tell lies about your next-door neighbours*, which would have been different.

The car pulled up outside school and Dad said *You getting out then* and I nodded but my body did not move. Dad's been giving False Evidence. *Hurry up* he snapped, watching the windscreen wipers slosh rain from side to side. I unfastened my seat belt. Climbed out of the car. Dad drove off without saying goodbye. And as the car sped down the lane, I raised my middle finger towards the sky. Two rings were wrapped around it instead of one, the white and brown stones almost touching. I swore at God and I swore at Moses. Then I tilted my hand and swore at Dad and broke rule five and it felt good. The car disappeared around a corner as I ran into school to find Sunya.

*   *   *

Mrs Farmer said *Because it's nearly Christmas, we will be starting work on the birth of Jesus*. Everyone groaned and I could tell that this school was the same as my last one. In London we did Jesus every December and we acted out the stable bit for all the mums and dads who must've got bored of seeing the same play over and over again. So far I have been a sheep and the back end of a donkey and the star of Bethlehem, but never ever a person. Mrs Farmer said *It is important to understand The True Meaning Of Christmas* and I quietly sang *We three kings of Leicester Square, Selling ladies underwear, It's fantastic, Loads of elastic, Why don't you buy a pair*. Sunya didn't even smile.

Mrs Farmer said *We are going to write the story of The Lord's birth from Jesus' point of view*. Jesus wouldn't have seen anything apart from the inside of Mary's tummy, lots of straw and a few hairy nostrils when the shepherds peeped into the cot. But then Mrs Farmer said *This is the Most*

Important piece of work you'll do all year. I want you to try your best so I can give it a good grade and show it to your mums and dads at Parents' Evening. I wrote four pages before Mrs Farmer said *Put your pens down.* Mum's going to love it, especially when the inside of Mary's tummy glows bright red with the light of the angel Gabriel, who in my story I have made a lady in case Dad reads it at Parents' Evening. If he thinks boys with green hair are gay, I don't know what he'd say about a man with wings.

I ripped a page out of my sketchbook and scribbled a note to Sunya. It said *Meet me in the storeroom at playtime* and I drew a smiley face that had devil's horns with my special pencils. She read the note but her face did not move. When we were allowed outside, I quickly ran to the receptionist's office but I didn't hold Mrs Williams at gun point and demand she hand over all the chocolate bars or anything. I bought a Crunchie with my money from Granny and then sprinted outside and disappeared through the hidden door.

I bounced a tennis ball fifty one times before I realised that Sunya wasn't coming. I was annoyed with her for being a sulky girl so I tore open the Crunchie and was about to take a big bite when I stopped myself. My mouth was watering like crazy but I wrapped the chocolate up again and put it down my sock 'cos I didn't have pockets in my trousers. In Maths I wrote Sunya another note and asked her to meet me in the storeroom at lunchtime. This time I put *Please* and *P.S. I've got a surprise for you* to try and make her come.

I ate my sandwiches sitting on a football. It kept rolling around and it was difficult to balance and I dropped one of my crusts on the floor. Every time something creaked, and even when nothing did, my heart exploded and my right leg twitched and my mouth felt too dry to swallow the bread. My eyes were glued to the crack of light by the door. I kept hoping that it would grow into a square and Sunya would be standing there, a silhouette against the sun, but the handle didn't turn and the door stayed closed.

I grabbed a tennis racquet and smacked a ball against the wall. I did it again. And again and again and again. Faster and harder every single time. Sweat trickled down my back and my breath was noisy and then there was a tap on my shoulder and I missed the ball and it whacked me in the face. Sunya said *Are you okay* and I knew it should have hurt but I didn't feel anything except happy to see her.

I nodded and took her ring off my middle finger. I held it out and she stared at it and stared at it and didn't say anything for a million years. So I said *Put it on then* and she said *Is that it* and I said *Is that what* and she shook her head and walked off. She was at the door when I shouted *Don't go* and she said *Why not* and I said *The surprise*. I pulled down my sock and offered her the Crunchie.

The look on her face was exactly the same as the one I gave Roger when he brought me the dead rabbit. She turned up her nose, stormed out of the storeroom and slammed the door in my face. The walls shook and everything went dark. I looked down at my hand. The Crunchie was all squished and gooey and there were bits of white fluff stuck in the melted chocolate.

I looked around the storeroom for something to give her. The only interesting-looking present was a javelin and that would have been too big to sneak out without being seen by the fat dinner lady. The storeroom was no fun on my own so I went outside into the rain and something yellow caught my eye. I had an idea.

There was ten minutes of lunchtime left. I walked around the playground trying to find Sunya with the new surprise hidden behind my back. I saw her with Daniel and for a millisecond I felt jealous but then I realised they were arguing. I stayed back 'cos I didn't want to get beaten up but I heard Daniel say *Curry Germs* and *You stink* before running off. I went over to her and my palms were all damp and my heart was jumping up against my ribs like Sammy the dog at Sunya's gate. I said *Ta da* and held out the flowers I'd just picked. And though most of them were dandelions, they looked really good so I was surprised when she started to cry.

Sunya is strong and Sunya is Girl M and Sunya is sunshine and smiles and sparkle. But this Sunya looked different and the dog in my chest had a droopy sad tail. *What's wrong* I asked and she just shook her head. Tears trickled down her cheeks one after the other after the other and she sniffed and bit her wobbly lip. I said *Do you want them then* and it came out too loud as if I was mad at her or something, when really I was just cross with Daniel for making her cry and ruining my surprise. She snatched the flowers out of my hand and threw them on the floor. Then she stamped on them as hard as she could and dragged her foot back so the petals smeared all over the playground. *I do NOT want your stupid flowers or your stupid chocolate* she shouted, and I was stuck 'cos I couldn't think of anything else to give her. So I said *Well, what do you*

100

want then and she yelled *For you to SAY SORRY*.

I looked at her then, really looked at her, and she glared back with a hurt that was big and raw and real. And all of a sudden my eyes could see all the bad things I'd done and my ears could hear all the nasty things I'd said. I remembered running away when she offered me the ring. I remembered saying *Just leave me alone* outside the Headmaster's office. I remembered walking off at Halloween, saying *Shut up* after football, and ignoring her for no reason after I'd been to her house. Well, not for no reason. I was trying to get into Heaven at the time, but that's not a good enough excuse.

I grabbed her hand and Daniel shouted *Sissy Spider-Man's caught Curry Germs* but I ignored him. I said *I'm sorry* and I meant it and Sunya nodded but did not smile.

14

I asked Sunya if she wanted to walk home but she said *No thanks*. She was my friend again 'cos she borrowed my special pencils to draw a map in Geography, but it didn't feel the same. I told three jokes including the number one most funny Knock Knock joke of all time and she didn't even laugh. And when I gave her the Blu-Tack ring in History, she put it in her pencil case instead of on her finger.

It took me ages to walk home. My feet and bag felt heavier than normal. Roger jumped out of a bush when I was two minutes from the cottage so I said *Sorry* to him as well. Hunting is what cats do and I shouldn't get mad when he kills stuff. He followed me home and we sat in the porch for a long time, my back against the door and Roger's back against the floor, his orange paws stuck up in the air. I dangled a shoe lace and he played with it and meowed like he'd forgotten all about our argument. I wish girls were as simple as cats.

The house felt different when I went inside. Empty. Dark. Rain splattered the windows and the radiators were freezing. Food wasn't cooking in the kitchen and Dad didn't say *How was your day*. Even though this has only happened a few times, I've started to get used to it so the grey silence scared me. I wanted to shout *Dad* but I was afraid of hearing nothing so I started to whistle and turn on the lights. I was worried there might be a note on the table in the kitchen saying *I can't do this any more*. There wasn't, but I couldn't see Dad anywhere either.

That's when I noticed the cellar door. It was open. Not much. Only a crack. It was dark down there. I flicked the light switch. Nothing happened. I kept thinking about Candyman so I got a wooden spoon out of the kitchen drawer, just in case. Then I realised that a wooden spoon wouldn't be much use against a hook and I swapped it for a corkscrew. I walked down the first step. My toes ached on the cold concrete. *Dad* I whispered. No answer. I walked down the second step. In the bottom of the cellar, I could see a yellow beam from a torch. *Dad* I said again. *Are you down there*. Someone was breathing heavily. I lowered my foot slowly onto step three but then I couldn't hack it any more and I charged.

We'd been robbed. That was the only

explanation. I couldn't even see the cellar floor it was covered by so much stuff. Photos and books and clothes and toys and Dad's legs dangling out of a big box. *How did they get in* I asked, balancing on the last step 'cos there was nowhere else to put my feet. I hadn't seen any smashed windows. *Who did this*. Dad was leaning right inside the box when I spotted the writing on the side of the cardboard. SACRED. Dad's arms were moving about and his hand found something and flung it over his head into the air and onto the floor. *You did* I whispered.

Dad popped out of the box. He looked pale in the light of the torch and his black hair was sticking up. A badge hung from his stained shirt saying I Am Seven Today. *Found it* he said, waving a painting in the air. *Brilliant, isn't it*. It wasn't even a picture, just five blobs on a crumpled piece of paper, but I bit my tongue and nodded. *They are so small, James. Look how small they are.*

I stepped over a shoe with a buckle and a small flowery dress and an old birthday card that had a badge missing. I leaned closer. The blobs turned into handprints. There were two big ones with Mum and Dad written inside, two small ones with Jas and Rose written inside, and a tiny one with my name inside. They were in a circle around a heart and in the heart someone had written Happy Father's Day. Probably Mum, 'cos it was all neat.

It's a nice picture but kissing it was a bit much. Dad's lips pressed against Jas's hands then Rose's hands then Jas's hands again. *Beautiful names* he said in this quivery voice that got on my nerves. *Jasmine and Rose.* He stroked the twins' old handprints. *This is how I remember them.* I felt confused and said *Jas's still alive*, but Dad didn't hear. His head had flopped into his hands and his shoulders were shaking. I got a strong urge to laugh 'cos he kept hiccupping really loud and really high but I swallowed it back down and tried to think of sad things like war and those kids in Africa that have fat bellies, even though they don't eat anything.

Dad was saying something but it was all covered in snot and tears so the only words I could make out were *Always* and *My little girls*. Jas is big and beautiful and pink and pierced and Dad is missing out if he wishes she was still ten years old.

Granny says *People always want what they can't have* and I reckon it's true. Dad wants Rose to be alive and Jas to be ten, but he's got me. I am the right age but the wrong sex, Jas is the right sex but the wrong age, and Rose is the right age and the right sex. But she is dead. *Some people are never satisfied* is something else Granny says.

Jas didn't come home until eleven so I had to do all the things she normally does. I cleaned the toilet after Dad was sick and I put him into bed. He tucked the Father's Day picture under the covers and something painful twisted in my tummy. He fell asleep quickly. His whole face wobbled as he snored and I got him a glass of water for later. I watched him for about a minute and then I went into my bedroom and sat on the windowsill with the information about Britain's Biggest Talent Show. Roger was purring so hard his throat felt warm and buzzy on my toes. The top of the letter said *Come to Manchester to change your life* and I imagined me and Jas going to the theatre and walking onto the stage and singing for the judges in front of loads of TV cameras. I could see Mum's face in the audience and she was sitting next to Dad and they were holding hands 'cos they were proud of us. They'd forgotten all about the arguments and they'd forgotten all about Rose and it didn't matter one bit that Jas had grown up and changed. After the competition, Mum phoned Nigel and said *I am leaving you.* She even called him a bastard and we all laughed and got into the same car and went back to the same house. Dad threw away his alcohol. Mum said *You look great in your t-shirt* and I could finally take it off and put on a pair of pyjamas. Then I lay in bed and Mum tucked me under the covers like she used to before she ran off with the man from the support group one hundred and sixty eight days ago.

*   *   *

Mrs Farmer walked into the classroom in a black suit that was too small. Her tummy hung over the top of the trousers and it looked pale and squidgy like pastry dough. She said *Good morning my dears* and it sounded different, too soft and too friendly. She said *Let's wake up our minds* and we had to stand up and do these strange things with our arms that make the different parts of our brains work really hard. I was just wondering if Mrs Farmer had gone mental when a man with a clipboard walked into the classroom. Mrs Farmer said *This is Mr Price and he is from Ofsted.*

On the board Mrs Farmer wrote something called a Learning Objective and went on and on about our target for the morning. I could tell she was trying to impress Mr Price from the way she kept glancing at him, but he didn't smile. He had long fingers and a long chin and a long nose with a pair of glasses right at the very end. We were doing Jesus again and we had to work in pairs and make the nativity scene out of clay. One person had to make the people and the crib and the other person had to do the stable and the animals.

Sunya made the cows and the sheep and a really fat animal that might have been a pig except for the fact it had a horn. Mrs Farmer walked past and did a double take and whispered *What on earth is that* and Sunya said *A rhino*. Mrs Farmer glanced over her shoulder to check Mr Price wasn't looking and then she bashed the clay animal with her fist. The rhino splattered onto the desk and Sunya's eyes flashed dangerously. *The birth of The Lord Jesus Christ did not take place in a zoo* Mrs Farmer hissed and Sunya said *How do you know*. The Ofsted Inspector walked over to our table and asked *And what are you making*. Sunya opened her mouth but Mrs Farmer yelled *Sheep* before Sunya had a chance to reply. *You are making sheep, aren't you dear*. Sunya didn't say anything but she rolled a bit of clay into a pointy sausage that looked exactly like a horn.

Mrs Farmer left and walked around the pairs saying *How are you getting on* and it felt weird 'cos she normally just sits at her desk and drinks coffee. Mr Price talked to Daniel and Ryan who were making a perfect stable with perfect animals and a perfect baby Jesus. Daniel was going on and on about Mrs Farmer being a good teacher, and Mrs Farmer was pretending that she couldn't hear, but she had two pleased pink circles on her cheekbones. Daniel looked over at the display as if he knew his post-it would soon be on cloud two.

Sunya rolled the clay fiercely, making five more horns.

Near the end of the lesson, Mrs Farmer took off her jacket. Two sweat patches dripped under her arms. She said *Excellent work my dears. Please put your stables on the front table and I will bake them in the oven at playtime.* Mr Price said *I would like to come back and see the models when they are finished* and Mrs Farmer blinked but said *That would be lovely.* The Inspector walked out of the room and Mrs Farmer flopped onto her chair and said *Tidy up this mess,* her voice back to normal.

Sunya took our stable to the front and leaned over to look at the other children's work. She was there for ages leaving me to do all the tidying up and I would have been annoyed if I wasn't trying so hard to be nice. When the classroom was clean, we were allowed outside, but Sunya disappeared into the girls' toilets and didn't come out again until the fat dinner lady blew the whistle.

While Jesus cooked in the oven, we did English. Mrs Farmer's eyes kept zooming to the door as if she expected the Inspector to come in at any moment. We wrote poems called My Magical Christmas and we had to include all the wonderful things we were looking forward to. I couldn't think of a single thing. Christmas is always sad in my family. Last year, Dad hung a stocking next to the urn and yelled at Mum when she didn't fill it with presents. And this year will be worse than ever 'cos Mum's not here to cook Christmas dinner, which is the best thing about the whole holiday, even if it does mean eating sprouts.

Mrs Farmer said *Hurry up, James* so I just started scribbling. I imagined the best Christmas ever and wrote about that instead. I described the warm turkey smells and the ringing church bells. I wrote about the matching grins of the happy pretty twins. I couldn't think of anything to rhyme with Santa except Fanta, which isn't my favourite drink like I said in verse two. But, as the whole poem is a great big lie, I don't think it matters.

For once Sunya was struggling and she only wrote four lines. I whispered *What's wrong* and she said *I don't celebrate Christmas*. I didn't know what to say to that. I can't imagine winter without Christmas except in that film Narnia where the White Witch stops Father Christmas delivering presents to the talking beavers. Sunya said *I wish I was normal* as Mr Price walked in.

The clay was ready so Mrs Farmer got it out of the oven. She said *Careful they are hot* as we all gathered round. Mr Price's nose poked over the top of the clipboard. Our stable looked good. Mary was bigger than Joseph, and Jesus' arms and right leg had fallen off so he looked like a tadpole, but apart from that it was perfect. None of the animals had horns and I was just wondering where Sunya had put the pointy sausages when Mr Price gasped. I followed his eyes and saw Daniel's stable. Inside, all the animals had something stuck to the middle of their foreheads. And not just the animals—Mary, Joseph, even baby Jesus had a sausage shape stuck between their eyebrows. I looked at Sunya. Her face was innocent but her eyes burned like coal. The pointy sausages looked nothing like horns. They looked like small willies. I put my hand over my mouth to stop myself laughing. I didn't dare look at Daniel in case he blamed me, but I thought *Who's the dickhead now*.

Mr Price left the room, his cheeks purple and the pen shaking in his long fingers as he wrote something bad on the clipboard. Daniel didn't get into trouble. Mrs Farmer had no proof it was him. It didn't matter though. We'd got revenge. The whole class had to stay in at lunchtime 'cos no one would own up to *Debasing the son of God*, whatever that means. Everyone was cross 'cos white flakes had started to fall from the sky and the other classes were in the playground having snowball fights. But I didn't mind 'cos this way I got to spend lunchtime with Sunya rather than waiting for her to come out of the girls' toilets.

Before Jas stopped eating, she used to love bangers and mash. She cut up all the sausages and hid them in the mashed potato. After school, that's what I thought of. Partly 'cos I was starving and partly 'cos the world looked like a huge plate of Jas's bangers and mash, everything hidden under lumpy white snow.

Sunya didn't wait when Mrs Farmer told the class to get out of her sight. She ran out of school and walked as fast as she could down the road. I slipped trying to catch up with her. When I shouted her name, she stopped and turned round. Her face was dark beneath the snowflakes and she looked so pretty I forgot what I was about to say. *What do you want, Jamie.* She didn't sound cross, just tired and fed up. Maybe even bored, and that was worse than anything. I went all cold and it had nothing to do with the snow. I wanted to say something really funny to make her eyes sparkle, but my mind had gone blank and I just stared and stared as the snow swirled all around us. After a long pause, I said *How many people have you saved today, Girl M* and

109

she rolled her eyes. I said *I've saved one thousand and four but it was a quiet day* and she folded her arms and sighed impatiently. Her hijab was dotted with snowflakes and it flapped in the wind. She looked annoyed so I said *Thank you* and she said *For what*. I took a step closer. *For giving Jesus a dickhead, for getting Daniel back* and in my head I added *For everything*. Sunya shrugged. *I didn't do it for you. I did it for me*. Then she turned around and walked off, her feet leaving deep prints in the snow.

15

I've been telling Dad all week that he has to come into school at 3.15pm tomorrow. I hope he doesn't drink. I don't want him to embarrass me or Mum. She never replied to the letter but I know that she'll come. I think she'll come. I really hope so. I crossed my fingers for one hour and thirteen minutes yesterday, just to make sure. Jas said *Don't get your hopes up* but I said *Mum won't miss Parents' Evening*. The story I wrote from Jesus' point of view got an A so now my angel is on cloud seven. I can't wait for Mum to read it.

When I got home from school earlier, the light on the answer machine was flashing. I thought it might be Mum leaving a message about tomorrow so I made myself wait to listen to it. Dad was asleep on the sofa with the urn on a cushion and the Father's Day picture tucked underneath his double chin, fluttering every time he breathed out. I closed the door and I fed Roger and I brushed my teeth and splashed my face and combed my hair with my

110

fingers. I hadn't heard Mum's voice for months and I wanted to look good. The Spider-Man top is all creased and mucky so I rubbed it down with a wet towel and sprayed it with my deodorant.

When I was ready, I dragged a chair to the phone and sat down, feeling nervous. I stretched out a finger. My hand flashed red in the light of the answer machine. It dangled above the Play button. I was desperate to hear Mum's voice, but suddenly terrified too. She might have phoned to cancel. I started to count to thirty but my finger bashed the button before I even got to seventeen.

A woman's voice. *Oh hello* it said, surprised to be talking to an answer machine. It didn't sound like Mum but then again people put on a different voice for the phone. I crossed my fingers.

Mr and Mrs Matthews, I am Miss Lewis, Jasmine's form tutor. Nothing to worry about but Jasmine hasn't been in school since last Friday. I wanted to make sure that she's at home with you. I'm assuming she hasn't been very well and that's why I've not seen her for a while. Could you please give me a call this afternoon to let me know where she's been and how she's doing. If Jasmine is off sick, I hope she gets better soon and that we see her in school in the next few days. Thanks very much.

My first thought was *It's not Mum it's not Mum it's not Mum* and I couldn't really concentrate on what Miss Lewis was saying. So I pressed Repeat and listened again, my jaw dropping a bit more with each sentence. Jas wasn't ill. She'd set off to school that morning in her uniform.

111

I sat there in silence, too shocked to move. Roger jumped onto my lap. His tail twisted through the air like one of those charmed snakes you see in dusty countries like Africa and on the film Aladdin. I didn't know what to do. Skiving school is serious.

Where have you been I asked when the handle turned and Jas walked into the hall. She looked at me like I was being stupid and said *School*. The lie slapped me in the face and my cheeks felt like the answer machine, flashing flashing flashing red. I said *Tell the truth* and she said *Don't be so nosy* in this sarcastic way. *Miss Lewis left a message* I said and Jas's eyes zoomed to the answer machine and her hand zoomed to her mouth. She said *Has Dad*—and I said *No* and she said *Will you*—and I said *Of course I won't tell him*.

She nodded and made herself a cup of tea and asked if I wanted a hot Ribena, which is just about my favourite drink but impossible to rhyme with Christmas words. I said *Yes* but not *Please*. I was still cross with her for telling lies and having adventures that didn't include me. She sat down at the kitchen table and said *I'm sorry* and I said *S'okay*, but it wasn't really and it annoyed me that she looked relieved, like just one little word had made it all go away. And I thought of Sunya and for the first time I understood why she didn't want to wear the Blu-Tack ring. She hadn't forgiven me 'cos I'd only apologised once and it wasn't enough.

I wanted to run out of the kitchen and all the way down the road and up the hill to Sunya's house. I wanted to stand outside her window and shout *Sorry sorry sorry* until she looked down with sparkly eyes and said *It's okay* and actually meant it. But I couldn't, so I didn't, and I just sat at the table and

112

waited for Jas to start talking.

I'm in love. I wasn't expecting that. I coughed Ribena down my t-shirt. Jas patted me on the back. When I could breathe again, I said *With Leo* and she bit her nails and I said *Oh.* Jas fidgeted on her seat. *What Dad said* she began, her eyes filling with tears. I stood up to get her a tissue but couldn't find one so I gave her a tea towel instead. She laughed when I handed it to her but it didn't sound happy. *What Dad said in the car. All that stuff about Leo being a girl. Being gay. I'll never forgive him.* I said *You have to forgive him* and she sniffed and asked *Why.* So I said *He's our dad* and she said *So what* and then I was stuck. *He's our dad* I repeated. I didn't know what else to say. And Jas said *And we're his kids.* I didn't understand what that meant so I squeezed her hand. It felt all cold and bony.

After Dad drove off and left me in the rain, I couldn't go to school. Jas was staring at a mark on the table as she talked. *I called Leo and he skived off college and picked me up. We spent the day together and it was the happiest I'd ever been. School didn't seem so important after that.* I shuffled a bit closer and shook my head. *School is important* I said. *Really important. Mum said good grades can get us anything that we want. Mum said education is—*

Jas looked away from the mark on the table and stared straight into my eyes. *Mum's not here, Jamie.*

I was going to tell her again about Parents' Evening, how Mum was probably packing a bag right at that moment, excited to see me. I wanted to say *Mum is coming. She'll be standing outside my school, Ambleside Church of England Primary, tomorrow at 3.15pm. Without Nigel.* But I didn't. I didn't say a word and I felt the first flicker of something that scared me.

I'll go back to school tomorrow Jas said. *I'll forge a note from Dad and it'll be okay.* And I said *Do you promise* and she said *Cross my heart and hope to*—but then stopped. We both thought of our dead sister on the mantelpiece and then Jas stood up and washed the cups in the kitchen sink. *I'm sorry* she said again as the washing up liquid made bubbles that looked like snow and sea foam and the fizz of Fanta. *For lying and skiving and stuff.* I said *It's okay* and this time I meant it. *It's just hard* she said as she scrubbed the cups. *To think of anything else. To keep away from him. You'll understand one day.* I didn't say anything, but I thought I understood just fine.

*   *   *

I apologised to Sunya over three hundred times. Whenever Mrs Farmer stopped talking I said *Sorry sorry sorry sorry sorry sorry sorry* without even taking a breath. For some reason it didn't work and she was all quiet and sad. At lunchtime we sat on our bench but Daniel shouted *Are you getting curry for Christmas, Curry Germs* and threw a snowball at her head. I wanted to say something but I didn't and Sunya ran off and spent the rest of lunch in the girls' toilets. I think Daniel knows it was Sunya who put the dicks in his stable 'cos he's being nastier to her than ever before.

I couldn't concentrate all day 'cos Mum was on her way. I couldn't do maps or Victorians or writing neatly in paragraphs. I just stared at my books and wrote nothing. I kept my pen in my hand so Mrs Farmer wouldn't shout at me and tell Mum I was a lazy boy. When school finished I felt tired, as if I'd been awake and waiting for 3.15pm for a million years.

My appointment was first. Mrs Farmer said *Go and meet your parents and I will be with you in five minutes*. I went outside and saw Dad's car and I was relieved when he whirred down the window and said *Hi* in a voice that wasn't too drunk. He said *What's wrong* 'cos my head kept twisting and my heart was banging and my knees were shaking and my mouth was dry. There were lots of cars in the carpark, but none of them contained Mum.

Dad said he needed the loo so we went inside. While he was in the boys' toilets, I ran out of the door and sprinted up the drive to double check the sign. It definitely said *Ambleside Church of England Primary* so Mum couldn't have driven past without seeing the school. My Spider-Man top was soaking 'cos of the snow and it stuck to my skin and looked stupid. The sleeves felt bigger than ever and goose bumps prickled against the red and blue material.

I waited and waited and waited. Snow fell heavily. Flakes stuck to my eyelashes. There was a gust of icy wind and I wrapped my arms around my chest. And then I heard a car.

A woman was driving. A woman with long hair, just like Mum's. I ran towards her, waving my hand. I slipped and fell over and my kneecap hit the snow, which had orange spots where the caretaker had sprinkled grit. The car indicated into the drive.

Mum I shouted. She had come. I felt so happy that I couldn't even move, even though I was still on my hands and knees in the snow on the road. *Mum.* The woman drove forward slowly, leaning over the steering wheel, the windscreen wipers moving quickly as snow fell on the glass. I waved again and looked into the car. The woman stared back, her eyes scrunched under glasses as though she was confused.

Mum doesn't wear glasses.

I looked again. Mum doesn't have brown hair either. The woman, someone else's mum, pointed to the pavement. She wanted me to move but I couldn't stand up, and it wasn't happiness but something much more scary that kept me on my knees. She beeped three times. I crawled to the side of the road.

Dad found me by a wall. He said *What the bloody hell are you doing* and grabbed me by the shoulder. He pulled me to my feet and I don't know how we got there 'cos my mind was three hundred miles away in London, but all of a sudden I was sitting in front of Mrs Farmer and she was saying I got an A for my story about Jesus' birth.

Mum had lied again. She said good grades can get me anything I want. But what I wanted was for her to be at Parents' Evening and she wasn't there.

Dad looked impressed and said *Can I see it*. He pretended to read a bit and then said *Well done,* but I felt nothing. Numb. And not 'cos of the snow. Mrs Farmer had a little heater under the desk and it had warmed my feet right up. Mrs Farmer said something, and Dad said something, and Mrs Farmer said something else then looked at me as if she expected an answer. So I said *Yes,* and I didn't even care that I hadn't heard the question. Mrs Farmer smiled so I must have said the right thing and then she asked *What secondary school will he be going to next year* and Dad said *Grasmere* and Mrs Farmer said *Is that where the twins go*. Dad said *Excuse me* and all of a sudden I was paying attention.

Is that where the twins go Mrs Farmer asked again and Dad rubbed a hand over his chin and the whiskers made a scratchy noise. *Twins* he said, as if he didn't understand, and Mrs Farmer looked confused and said *Rose and—oh what's the other one called* and Dad didn't speak and I didn't speak and the wind howled outside.

Jas goes to Grasmere Dad said at last. I wanted to kick Mrs Farmer on the shin to stop her from speaking but that type of thing only works in books. *And how about Rose* she asked.

Dad said *Rose has gone to a better place* and Mrs Farmer asked *A private school* and Dad swallowed but didn't reply. Mrs Farmer went red and said *Well, anyway* and she grabbed my pile of work and started flicking through it. *James has written some beautiful pieces about your family*. She pulled out my English book and I wanted to shout *NOOOOO*, but Mrs Farmer had already passed it to Dad. He read My Wonderful Summer Holiday, Our Brilliant Family and My Magical Christmas and the book shook in his hand. Mrs Farmer waited for Dad to say *Well done*. She stared at me as I stared at Dad and Dad stared at the lies I'd written about Rose.

There was a noise outside the door. The next parents had arrived. Mrs Farmer cleared her throat and said *To sum up, James is bright and sometimes works well, though he does tend to daydream. Socially, I'd like to see him mix a little more with the other children, but he seems particularly close to a girl called Sunya*. There was a knock on the door. *A girl called Sonya* Dad repeated and Mrs Farmer said *Come in. Not Sonya, Mr Matthews. Sunya*.

The handle clicked. The door opened. *Oh, here's Sunya now* Mrs Farmer announced cheerfully. I spun around in my chair, the Spider-Man t-shirt stuck to the sweat on my back. *Hello, Jamie* Sunya's mum said in her funny accent. *Nice to see you again.*

16

Two white hijabs glowed in the light of the classroom. Two dark faces looked shocked as Dad leapt to his feet. *How do you know my son* he yelled, banging his hand on Mrs Farmer's desk. A pile of books fell over and knocked a cup of coffee onto some important-looking papers. Mrs Farmer made a noise like a frightened dog and looked at me as though it was my fault. Sunya's mum went *Erm* and I shook my head the tiniest amount so she said *I don't know him*. I closed my eyes and opened them slowly and I hoped Sunya's mum knew that it meant *Thank you.*

I whispered *Let's go* but Dad shouted *Nice to see you again. AGAIN. That's what you said.* He walked over to Sunya's mum. She took a step backwards and grabbed Sunya's shoulder. Mrs Farmer stood up, her hand flying to her chest. *Mr Matthews, calm yourself* she squeaked. Dad shouted over her. *Where have you seen him before.* Sunya's mum took another step back, dragging Sunya with her. *When did you meet my son.* Sunya shook off her mum's hand and said *At the school football match* and her voice was calm and her face was innocent and the lie was the best I had ever seen. *Shut up* Dad yelled and Sunya's mum suddenly exploded. *How dare you* she said, her eyebrows disappearing underneath the white hijab. *How dare you talk to my daughter like that*. Dad laughed but it sounded evil, like when a baddie rubs his hands together and his eyes go all red and the sound that comes out of his mouth is *HAHAHAHAHA*. *I can say what I want in my own country* Dad replied. I wanted to shout *It's Sunya's country too* but Dad looked mad. Mrs Farmer squeaked *I'm getting the Headmaster* and she smashed the door against the wall as she ran out of the classroom.

Muslims killed my daughter Dad said, pointing at his chest. I ran over to Dad and tried to grab his arm but he pushed me away. *They killed my daughter* he said again, jabbing his ribs on every syllable. *That's ridiculous* Sunya's mum replied, but her voice was shaky and I knew that she was scared. I thought about the curly straw in the chocolate milkshake and I hated Dad for frightening her. *Real Muslims would never, ever harm anything. Just because someone calls themselves a*—she started but Dad shouted *SHUT UP*. He was trembling now and his face was purple. Sweat dripped off his temples and ran down his cheeks. He yelled something about *Terrorists* and something else about *All the same* and Sunya's mum turned her head as if she had been slapped.

Sunya stood in front of a Christmas display, her fingers screwed up in tight fists. Snowflakes cut out of silver paper twinkled on the wall behind her. There were angels on the left and a Father Christmas on the right and his belly was bursting out of his red jacket and presents were bursting out of his black sack. In the middle of the display was a Mary cut out of blue cardboard and a Joseph cut out of brown cardboard and a baby Jesus cut out of cardboard that was too pink to look like skin. And it made me so sad to see Sunya next to all the Christmas things she didn't believe in and couldn't enjoy, and I thought about her poem and how she'd only written four lines 'cos there was nothing magical for her to look forward to in December. And even though Dad was still shouting and wind shook the windows and coffee drip drip dripped off the desk and formed a puddle on the floor, all I could hear were Sunya's words. *I wish I was normal.* I wanted to walk over to her and take her fists in my hands and put the ring back on her finger and say *I'm pleased you're not.*

A tear glittered in Sunya's left eye. It swelled silver like a fat raindrop as Dad called her family *Evil.* I imagined shouting *Don't listen to him.* I imagined saying *You are just different and it is beautiful.* And I imagined smashing Dad's face in for making Sunya cry, and for one millisecond I thought I might actually do it. But I just stood there in the middle of the classroom with my heart pounding and my body shaking in the Spider-Man top that was too big for a boy like me.

The Headmaster walked into the room, his shiny shoes tapping on the floor. He said *Is there a problem.* Sunya's mum didn't speak and all I could see was the top of her hijab as she stared at the ground. I wanted her to look up so I could say *Sorry* with my eyes but she didn't move. Dad said *No problem at all* and then grabbed my hand and pulled me towards the door and nodded at the Headmaster as though the last five minutes hadn't happened. I hoped that the bad stuff was over, but as we walked down the corridor, Dad's fingernails dug into the palm of my hand and it hurt. I was in trouble.

We didn't speak in the car. The tyres spun on the snow and white slush sprayed everywhere. As soon as we pulled into the drive, Dad whispered *Get inside* so I jumped out and slipped on the ice and burst through the front door and ran into the lounge. Jas and Leo were lying on the sofa, their faces all red and their black clothes crumpled. Jas said *I thought you had Parents' Evening* and I said *Finished* and *Dad* and pointed outside. Jas pushed Leo off the sofa with a scream.

Dad marched down the hall. *Quick* I said, tugging Jas's hand. Leo chewed on the ring through his lip. The footsteps stopped. *Hide* Jas hissed. The door handle turned. Leo dived behind the sofa as Dad walked into the lounge.

I am not that good at Hide And Seek. I don't like small dark places. They make me think of being buried underground so I panic and end up behind a door or somewhere rubbish. But even I am better at hiding than Leo, who didn't even make himself small enough to fit behind the sofa. His green spikes stuck over the top of the armrest and his black boots stuck out on the carpet.

When Dad saw him, his face went from purple to black and he yelled *Get up*. I don't think Leo knew that Dad was talking to him 'cos he just stayed there for ages, holding his breath and closing his eyes as if he thought he hadn't been seen. But then Dad walked over to the sofa and grabbed the back of Leo's t-shirt and pulled hard. Leo scrambled to his feet as Dad shouted *Get out of my house*. Jas said *Don't talk to him like that* and Dad said *I'll talk to him however I damn well like under my roof* and he

121

pointed at the ceiling with a shaky finger.

Leo ran off and Dad shouted *You are banned from my house and you are banned from seeing Jasmine.* He slammed the lounge door. An old picture of the family fell off the wall and smashed. *You can't do that* Jas said, furious and fiery, waving her hands around in the air. *You can't stop us from seeing each other.* Dad said *I think I just did* and then he turned to me.

Do you love Rose he asked and I said *Yes* straightaway. Dad took a step forward. *Do you remember how she died.* His voice was low and quiet and dangerous. I swallowed but there was no spit in my mouth. I nodded my head. Dad closed his eyes and seemed to be trying to control something but it was too strong for him 'cos he started to shout and kick the sofa. *LIAR. YOU'RE A LIAR, JAMES.* I squashed myself against the wall. Dad threw a cushion and it hit the light shade, which swung and creaked. *I'm not a liar* I replied, falling to my knees as Dad charged across the carpet. The urn rattled on the mantelpiece. *How can you do it then* Dad yelled, his voice booming in my ears like an iPod turned up loud. *If you're telling the truth, how can you be friends with that girl.*

Jas said *Leave him alone* and crawled to my side. She was crying and her arm shook as it wrapped around my shoulders. *Did you know about this* Dad roared, leaning over Jas and shouting in her face. *Did you know that Jamie's girlfriend is a Muslim.* Jas looked at me but she wasn't disappointed or angry, just curious, and she gave me a secret squeeze that said *I don't care. An effing TERRORIST* Dad yelled, splattering his chin with spit. I wanted to tell Dad that he was wrong, 'cos all the terrorists I have seen on TV are men over twenty not girls under eleven, but Dad thumped the wall just above my head and I had to hide my face.

My eyes were pressed into my kneecaps but I could hear that Dad was crying. He sniffed and snot rushed from his nostrils to his throat so when he spoke it sounded thick and sticky. *You never cry about her* he said and I felt guilty then, like every single thing that had gone wrong in my family was my fault. I poked myself in the eye to make them water.

You can't love her Dad said, his voice suddenly quiet. I peeped through my fingers. Dad walked over to the mantelpiece and stared at the urn. *Not if you wrote all those lies, pretending she's still alive when she's been dead for five years. Not if you're friends with a Muslim.* He took the urn off the mantelpiece and it trembled in his hands and his sweaty fingers left marks on the gold. *Look what they did to her, James* he said, holding up the urn. *Look what Muslims did to your sister.* He didn't seem angry any more, just sadder than the saddest person I can think of, which right now is Spider-Man when Uncle Ben dies. Jas cried even harder and I wished my eyes could do it too.

Everything went silent and I knew that it was over but I didn't know if it was okay to start speaking again. So I sat with my back to the wall and my palm stung and my head ached and I watched the hands of the clock tick round in a circle. After three minutes and thirty one seconds, Dad put the urn back on the mantelpiece and wiped his eyes and walked out of the lounge. I heard a glass tinkle and the clunk-fizz of a can being opened. Jas pulled me to my feet and said *Let's go to your room.*

We sat on the windowsill and stared at the stars. The twins were up there and so was the lion. The silver in the sky shone on all the snow, turning the grass into diamonds. *My horoscope said today was going to be awful* Jas said. *I didn't think it'd be this bad though.* Her breath made steamy circles on the glass. In the condensation she wrote a big J and then her name, and used the same J to write my name. All the letters dripped together and it looked cool. She said *You okay* and I said *Yeah.*

I miss Mum Jas said suddenly and it was strange 'cos I'd just been thinking the same thing. *I wish she was still here.* I stared at the floor. *She wasn't at Parents' Evening* I said in a small voice. Jas leaned back against the window. *I didn't think she would be.* I rubbed the carpet with my toes. *But maybe she got stuck on the motorway* I said. *If there was a traffic jam, she'd have given up and gone home. You know what she's like. Maybe that's what happened.* Jas fiddled with a strand of pink hair. *Maybe* she said, but we didn't look at each other. That flicker came back, like one of those trick birthday candles you just can't blow out. I didn't recognise the feeling but, whatever it was, it scared me.

We were silent for a while. Roger tiptoed across the garden, his orange feet leaving twinkling holes in the snow. He stared into the frozen pond. I wondered if my fish was alive somewhere underneath all the ice. Jas sighed. *I hope Leo's okay.* I picked a thread off the cushion and said *I hope Sunya is too.* Then I smiled, even though it wasn't funny. *Dad must really hate us.*

Yeah Jas said, crumpling her forehead. *And Mum.* I'd only meant it as a joke, and was about to say so when Jas rested her chin on her knees, all

124

thoughtful and serious. *When I was little, I had five teddies. Edward, Roland, Bertha, John and Burt.* I didn't understand why she was telling me about her toys. *My bear was called Barney* I said slowly. Jas drew five lines in the condensation on the glass. The black polish was chipped where she'd been biting her nails. *I loved them all. Especially Burt, who had no eyes. But one day I lost him. I left him on a bus in Scotland when we went to visit Granny and I never saw him again.* Roger disappeared under a bush, hunting. I banged on the window to make him stop. *I was so upset* Jas went on. *Cried for hours. But I was relieved to get back to my other bears in London.* She rubbed one of the lines off the glass and stared at the other four. *I loved them more than ever, 'cos there was one less.*

It was a pointless story so I didn't know what to say. I kept quiet and waited. *Maybe that's how they'll feel too* she said. *One day. When all the hurt goes away.* I didn't know if she was talking about the bears or Mum and Dad, but she looked young, not like my big sister at all, and I wanted her to feel nice so I just said *They will.* Jas squeezed her knees to her chest. *You really think so* she said and I nodded in a wise way. She smiled shakily and spoke all in a rush. *Then they'll love us for us without thinking about Rose and Mum'll come home and it'll all be okay.*

We can make her come home I said suddenly, jumping off the windowsill. *We can make her come home and everything will be okay.* I handed her the crumpled envelope hidden underneath my pillow. She opened it up and this time when she read the words *Come to Manchester to change your life*, she didn't say *What a load of crap* or anything like that.

She listened to my plan. I got to the bit where we walk into the theatre after singing our song and Mum and Dad are holding hands 'cos they're so proud, and this time she didn't say *That would never happen*. She whispered *I'd love it if they made up* and closed her eyes, imagining their first hug.

Let's do it then I said, feeling excited. *The audition's in three weeks. That's loads of time to get a talent*. Jas's eyelids had black powder all over them. They suddenly crumpled, as if she was in pain. *I can't cope with Dad any more. All the*—she hesitated and took a deep breath—*drinking*. It was the first time either of us had said that word and actually meant alcohol and sick and disappointment rather than hot Ribena or something. I was glad Jas had her eyes closed 'cos I didn't know what to do with my face or my hands or the enormous truth that our dad was a drunk.

I'm only fifteen she said loudly, opening her eyes suddenly and looking fierce. *You really want to enter that crap contest* she asked. I nodded my head and, after a pause, my sister said *Okay*.

17

The last week of term was rubbish. Sunya wasn't talking to me and I got sick of the snowballs Daniel threw at my face and the ice he put down my Spider-Man top and the fact that everyone got Christmas cards except me. There was this letterbox in the library and you pushed your cards inside and at the end of the day they got delivered to people in the class. The Headmaster would do it with a Santa hat on and he'd come into our room and say *Ho ho ho*. Then he'd read out the names on the cards in his hand and there were always loads for Ryan and loads for Daniel and quite a few for Sunya. This confused me at first 'cos Sunya's been standing on her own in the playground so I was surprised she was that popular. But then I saw that all her cards were drawn in felt tips on A4 paper and were signed in her handwriting by superheroes. She sent herself one from Batman and one from Shrek and one from The Green Goblin, who everyone knows is Spider-Man's biggest enemy. She put that one by her pencil case so I could see it.

We haven't spoken since Parents' Evening and she won't use my special pencils any more. There is so much I want to tell her about Britain's Biggest Talent Show and our plan to send a letter to Mum and leave a note for Dad to tell them to come to Manchester Palace Theatre on January 5th. I want to sing her our song and show her our dance moves and tell her that they will solve everything. When Mum's back and Dad's stopped drinking and they've forgotten all about Rose, Dad'll be too happy to hate Sunya. He might not like us being friends but Mum'll say *Just leave them alone* and Sunya will come round for tea. We will eat tropical pizzas and they will forget that she's a Muslim.

It's Christmas Eve in two days. I don't think the post comes on December 24th or December 25th or December 26th and there was nothing this morning apart from one of those sad letters from a charity that asks you to think of all the starving people in Africa while you're eating your turkey. I will try to remember them when I have my Christmas Dinner, which is going to be chicken sandwiches this year

127

'cos Jas's making it. I don't think the charity people will mind what I eat as long as I *Spare A Thought For Those Dying Of Hunger* while I am at the table.

If there's no post over Christmas then that leaves tomorrow for Mum to send a present. I'm trying to get excited. I keep imagining a fat parcel on the mat by the front door, but every time I think of the card with Happy Christmas Son in big blue letters, I get that weird flicker of something that scares me. It never really goes away now.

I asked Mrs Farmer how much warning she'd have to give the Headmaster if she needed a day off. She looked annoyed that I was talking to her and kept glancing at the display above her desk as if all the coffee splashes on the angels were my fault. Eventually she said *If it was important enough, I'd be allowed time off straightaway. Now go outside and play and stop asking silly questions.*

If it was important enough. I couldn't get those words out of my head. They whizzed round my brain and made me dizzy. When we wrote stories my pen didn't touch the paper and when we did Maths I made up the numbers and when we did Art I drew the lambs bigger than the shepherds 'cos I wasn't concentrating. It looked like a herd of killer sheep was going to trample over the crib.

For the school play surprise surprise we acted out the stable bit and I was a person for the first time ever. I got the part of the man who said *No room at the inn* but no one came to watch so it didn't matter. Jas couldn't get back from school in time and Dad hasn't been out of bed since Parents' Evening. Sunya got the part of Mary at first but she wouldn't stop groaning and holding her belly as if she was giving birth when she walked up to the inn.

In the last rehearsal, Mrs Farmer pulled Sunya off the chair in the middle of the stage and made her get on all fours and told her that she was an ox and to keep at the back of the stable.

On the very last day, I was desperate to talk to Sunya, but I couldn't think how to get started. When she wasn't looking, I chucked my pencil underneath her chair and was about to ask her to pick it up when Mrs Farmer sent me out for throwing sharp objects around the classroom. She said *You could have poked someone's eye out*, which was a lie. The pencil was blunt and anyway I threw it really low so, unless there was an invisible midget walking around, it didn't go near anyone's eyes. When I was allowed back into the classroom, the pencil was still by Sunya's feet, but I didn't dare ask for it 'cos Mrs Farmer had made it obvious that I'd chucked it there on purpose. I had to do my graph in pen and I plotted it all wrong and I couldn't rub it out so I will get a bad mark. Doesn't matter though. I am not interested in As any more. Jas was right about school. It's not that important really.

When it was time to go, Mrs Farmer said *Merry Christmas and a Happy New Year. School starts again on January 7th so I will see you all then.* Time was running out to make friends so I stayed in the classroom as everyone left and watched Sunya pack away. She took ages over it, putting her books in a neat pile and making sure her felt tips had their lids on and were in the packet in rainbow order. I got the feeling she was waiting for me to speak but she was humming really loud and Granny always says *It's rude to interrupt*. Five strands of hair were dangling over her face and she kept brushing them out of her eyes. Words like *Perfect* and *Shiny* and

Beautiful flew around my head but before I could say anything, Sunya walked off. She went to get her coat and I followed and she ran down the corridor and I followed and she burst out of the door and onto the drive but stopped when I yelled *OY*.

It wasn't the nicest word I could have said but it got her attention. She turned around. Most people had gone and it was already dark but Sunya's hijab glowed like fire in the orange streetlights. I wanted to say *Happy Christmas* but Sunya doesn't celebrate it so I said *Happy Winter* instead. She looked a bit confused and I panicked that maybe she didn't celebrate the seasons either. She started walking backwards and she was getting further and further away and I didn't want her to disappear into the night so I shouted the first thing that came into my head. *HAPPY RAMADAN*.

Sunya stopped moving. I ran up to her and held out my hand and said it again. *Happy Ramadan*. The words were hot in the frosty air and each syllable steamed. Sunya stared at me for a long time and I smiled hopefully until she said *Ramadan was in September*. I was scared I'd offended her but then her eyes started to sparkle and the freckle by her lip twitched as if she was about to smile. The bracelets tinkled. She lifted her arm. My fingers trembled as her hand moved towards mine. They were twenty centimetres apart. Ten centimetres apart. Five centi—

Someone beeped a horn and Sunya jumped and gasped *Mum*. She ran up the gritted path and got into the car. The door slammed shut. The engine started. Two twinkling eyes stared at me out of the front window. My fingers were still trembling as the car disappeared down the dark road.

Jas bought me loads of little Christmas presents, a Man Utd ruler and rubber and a new can of deodorant 'cos I had run out. She wrapped them all up and put them in one of my football socks so it looked like a stocking. I made her a photo frame out of cardboard and stuck the only picture I could find of us two inside it. No Mum. No Dad. No Rose. Just me and Jas and I surrounded us in black and pink flowers 'cos she's a girl and they are her favourite colours. And I got her a box of her favourite chocolates to make her eat something as she is too skinny.

We made chicken sandwiches with stuffing and microwave chips and we ate it in front of Spider-Man. It wasn't as good as I remember from my birthday but I still enjoyed it, especially the bit when Spider-Man beats up The Green Goblin. Roger nibbled bits of my sandwich but Jas didn't touch hers. *Saving room for my chocolates* she said, and she ate three of them later, which made me feel nice. She kept glancing out of the window with a sad look on her face, but every time I noticed, she changed it to a grin.

Mum didn't send any presents and Dad has no idea what day it is 'cos he just lies in bed and drinks and snores and drinks and snores so he didn't give us anything either. The only thing he did all Christmas was bang on the bedroom floor and shout *Stop making that racket* when we were singing carols as loud as we could.

At nine o'clock there was a tap on the window and Jas looked at me and I looked at her and we both crept to the curtain. For a millisecond I thought it might be Mum knocking on the glass and I felt annoyed with my heart for beating faster when I knew that it wouldn't be her. We moved the curtain out of the way and Jas's breath tickled my ear. I couldn't see anything, just snow in the front garden, but when my eyes got used to the dark I could see a sentence written in all the white. I Love You. Jas squeaked as if it was for her and I felt disappointed 'cos that meant it wasn't for me.

She pulled on Dad's wellies and tiptoed outside and she looked funny with her pink hair and green dressing grown, dragging through the snow. I pressed my face against the window and watched her find the card that Leo had left in the garden. I saw the way her eyes shone and her smile burned and her heart swelled in her chest like a cake rising in the rusty oven we use for cooking at school. She kissed the card as if it was the best thing ever and it got me thinking.

It took me two hours to make. With my special pencils, I drew lots of snowflakes and a snowman that looked like me and a snowman that looked like her and I covered the whole thing in glitter. Roger sat next to me as I worked on my bedroom floor and he kept getting in the way so now he has silver sparkles in his tail. It was easier to write in the card than talk to Sunya's face, so I put down all the things that I've wanted to say since the very beginning. Things like *Thank you for being my friend* and *I like looking at your freckle* and *Dad is a bully but I am not like him so please wear the Blu-Tack ring*. I told her all about the audition and how everything would be perfect once Mum came home and sorted Dad out and how we could be friends after January 5th. Even though I was running out of room, I invited her to come to Manchester Palace Theatre to watch the talent show and said that she would be amazed by Jas's singing and impressed by my dance moves. I signed the card from the only superhero she didn't get one from at school. Spider-Man.

I had to wait for Jas to go to sleep before I could sneak out and post it. The first time I crept into her room to see if her eyes were closed she was whispering into her mobile phone and said *Get out you spying little bastard*. But the second time I checked she was fast asleep with her hand dangling off the bed and her mouth open and her pink hair in a tangle on the pillow. The wind chime tinkled as I gently closed her door.

It was eleven o'clock when I put on my wellies. Roger rubbed his orange fur against the red rubber like he knew we were about to have an adventure. His green eyes looked wider than normal as we tiptoed towards the front door. *Sssh* I said 'cos he started to purr. In the quiet cottage it sounded as loud as a truck's engine. The door creaked as I opened it and the snow crunched as I trod on it, but nobody heard and I walked down the drive without being seen.

It felt so naughty to be outside on Christmas night, I kept expecting police sirens to start screaming and blue lights to start flashing and someone to shout *You are under arrest*. But nothing happened. Everything was silent. All I could see was the moon bouncing off the frosty tops of black mountains. I was free.

I felt giddy and I started to laugh and Roger looked at me as though I was mental. I felt like

133

there was no one in the whole world except me and my cat and we could do anything that we wanted, anything at all. I danced on the spot and waved my hands in the air and wiggled my bum and no one saw. I spun on the spot, faster and faster, the snow a white blur that zoomed past my eyes. I jumped on a wall and walked across it, my smile bigger than it had been since I scored the winning goal. The card flapped in the breeze and I imagined Sunya reading it, maybe even kissing the place where I'd written Spider-Man.

That made me feel I could fly so I leapt off the wall and flapped my arms and for a millisecond I actually hovered above the snow before landing on one foot. My blood fizzed like Coke at a party and my body tingled and I had more energy than ever in my life. Roger said *Meow*, and I said *I know what you mean* and I told him I'd meet him back at the cottage. I kissed his wet nose and his whiskers tickled my lips. Then I ran off as fast as I could and the cold wind stung my cheeks.

My hands slapped against Sunya's gate. I was panting and my pulse was racing and my feet were aching and my sweat was pouring. This was the bravest thing I had ever done ever and I grinned as I pushed open the gate and ran up Sunya's drive. When I jumped over the fence, I flew for a bit before landing in the back garden. I was a bird and Wayne Rooney and Spider-Man, all rolled into one, and there was nothing that scared me, not even Sammy the dog who had started growling in the kitchen.

I put the card on the lawn and grabbed a stone. I threw it at Sunya's window but it hit the wall two metres below. I picked up another. This one went flying over the roof. In books they always make it sound dead easy to hit the glass but it took me eleven goes. When the pebble tapped the window, I ran away and hid behind a bush 'cos I wanted to watch Sunya find the card. I counted to one hundred. Nothing happened. Sammy the dog was going crazy, barking and scratching and snarling, but I didn't care. I found a bigger rock and this time it was perfect and hit the window hard.

I sprinted back into the bush, cutting my cheek on a thorn, but it didn't sting one bit. This time I only had to count to thirteen. A curtain twitched and a dark face appeared at the window. A light came on.

The dark face was a man's. Sunya's dad said something over his shoulder to a person I couldn't see. He stared at the patio and the trees and the lawn and Sammy was growling and I was scared they'd let him out and he would find me in the bush.

Sunya's dad didn't see the card. After five minutes checking for burglars, he closed the curtains and turned off the light and Sammy barked for a bit but then he was quiet. I didn't dare move and I stayed as still as I could, even though a twig was digging into my leg and I had pins and needles in my right foot. I stared at the window and I didn't blink so my eyes dried up. I wanted Sunya to open the curtains and I wanted her to find the card and I wanted to make her happy 'cos she's been so sad at school. I thought about her hand and my hand and how they had almost touched, and I wondered what would have happened if her mum hadn't beeped the horn.

After about a million years, I thought it was safe to move. A church clock struck midnight as I

135

crawled out of the bush and the branches snapped and the sleeve of my t-shirt ripped. When I picked up the card, it was all soggy. Snow had soaked right through the envelope. I was just wondering if I should leave it, or take it back home, or post it through Sunya's letterbox, when I heard the door of the kitchen slide open.

I should've run or I should've hid or I should've dropped to the floor and covered myself in snow, but my body wouldn't move. My back was facing the house so I had no idea who was there and I jumped when a wet tongue licked my hand. Sammy wagged his tail and it beat against my shaking leg. I counted to three and turned around and there she was. Her scarf was wrapped around her hair but not as tight as normal. It looked like she had just done it dead quick. She was wearing blue pyjamas and I could see her toes and they were tiny and brown and straight and they looked nice on the kitchen floor.

She stared at me and I stared at her but she didn't smile. I said *Hello* and she put her finger to her lips to tell me to be quiet. I walked over to her and my arms felt too long and my legs felt too clumsy and my face felt too hot. I held out the card but she didn't look happy like Jas had done. I said *This is a card especially for you and I made it out of paper and glitter,* just in case she didn't realise how special it was. She didn't say *Thank you,* or *Wow,* or squeak like girls do when they're happy. She said *Sssh* and looked over her shoulder as if she was scared someone might see.

I forced it into her hand and waited for her to open the envelope. If she saw the snowman in the Spider-Man top and the snowman in the hijab, I knew she'd find it funny and smile. But she hid

136

the card under her pyjamas and whispered *You have to go*. When I didn't move, she looked over her shoulder again and said *Please just go. I am not allowed to be friends with you. My mum thinks you're bad news*. I said *WHAT* and she put her hand over my mouth. My lips burned like they did on Halloween. A floorboard creaked upstairs. She said *Go* and pushed me away and she grabbed Sammy by the collar and pulled him inside. A light came on as I ran through the snow and Sunya closed the kitchen door. And this time when I jumped over the garden fence, I fell rather than flew and I hit the cold earth with a bang.

18

I dropped my Coco Pops when Jas walked into the kitchen. I hardly recognised her. *You look like—* I started and she said *Shut it* and *Find me a pen*. It took her ten goes to write a message to Dad. One said *Please please please come* but that sounded desperate so the next one said *Be there or else*, which was a bit too threatening. After eight more attempts, she finally wrote *Dad. We have a surprise for you and would love it if you came to Manchester Palace Theatre today. Be there at 1pm for the show of a lifetime*.

I was more nervous than the most nervous person I can think of, which right now is the lion in The Wizard of Oz. My tummy had something bigger and scarier than butterflies inside it. Maybe they were eagles or hawks or something. Or now I come to think of it they could have been those monkeys with wings that kidnap Dorothy and take her to the witch that's scared of water. Whatever they were they kept biting at my skin and swooping about not in a nice way. I was scared I'd forget everything and mess it all up so I kept running through the words and the dance moves as Jas wrote the message. That's why she had to get rid of the sixth attempt at Dad's letter. I knocked her pen with my leg as I did a high kick. For some reason that made me laugh and she looked annoyed and whispered *Bloody hell, Jamie*. And then she wouldn't let me help her put the letter on Dad's bedside table or set the alarm in his room for quarter past seven in case I was too noisy.

It was five o'clock in the morning and we were being quiet, even though there was no need. Dad doesn't wake up in the middle of the day when the TV's blasting in the lounge. But we still tiptoed about and our hearts went BOOM if one of us dropped something or spoke too loud. Jas was scared 'cos Leo was picking us up in his car and she didn't want Dad to see and go mental. I was scared 'cos if Dad found out and stopped us from going then he'd never get back together with Mum. We'd sent her a letter on December 28th so it has had plenty of time to get there. And Mr Walker's no excuse this time. The college is closed at Christmas. I made the competition sound really important and kept writing *Once in a lifetime opportunity*, which I had heard on TV, and *Come to Manchester to change your life*, which I stole from the letter, and *Please Mum I really need to see you*, which I just made up myself.

I can't believe I'm doing this Jas said as we went into the lounge to wait for Leo. *My horoscope said not to take a risk today.* She breathed shakily with her hand on her chest. *Let's go through it one more time* I said, watching her fingers tremble. We whispered the words and did the dance moves but Roger had woken up and kept getting in the way. He was twisting his body around my feet so I couldn't jump or stamp or run around Jas like I have to do in verse one. He was getting on my nerves but I was trying not to say anything 'cos I still felt bad for slamming the door in his face. When I tripped over his sparkly tail though, I lost it a bit. I leaned down and he looked at me all hopeful as if he was about to get a stroke. But instead of rubbing his fur, I picked him up and took him into the hall and shut him out of the lounge. He kept meowing at the door but I ignored him and eventually he got bored and ran off.

He's here Jas squeaked. A blue car pulled up outside the cottage. She fiddled with her new hair and said *Is it okay.* I said *Yes,* even though it looked strange. She must have dyed it brown last night and it was tied neatly in two short plaits. She looked so like Rose it was weird. I know they were identical and everything, but Jas just looks like Jas now. When I got into Leo's car, it was like Rose's spirit had come down from that cloud in Heaven and I missed the piercings and pink hair and black clothes. Jas was wearing a flowery dress, a cardigan and flat shoes with buckles, the last clothes Mum had bought her in London. I was still in my Spider-Man t-shirt 'cos Mum would be disappointed if I turned up not wearing it. I'd made it as smart as possible by wiping it with a cloth and fixing my sleeve with safety pins.

Leo raised his eyebrows when he saw Jas. She

looked at him with her face all stressed and said *It's just for today* and Leo looked relieved but said *You look cute*. Then Jas laughed and he laughed and I felt left out so I laughed, and then we were on our way. We drove fast 'cos the letter said it was first come first served and only one hundred and fifty acts would have time to go on stage. We sped through mountains and the sun rose as we climbed up hills and zoomed past farms and wiggled down country lanes. At one point we were driving right into the sun and the car was filled with this orange-yellow light and it was warm, like being inside an egg yolk or something. And everything looked beautiful and everything felt hopeful and all of a sudden I couldn't wait to get on stage.

*   *   *

A girl with a clipboard came up to us when we arrived and said *What is your act* and Jas said *Singing and dancing* and the girl sighed as though it was the most boring thing she had ever heard. She gave us a number, which was one hundred and thirteen, and said *Be ready at 5pm to perform. You will get three minutes on stage, or less if the judges don't like you.* I looked at the clock on the wall. It was ten past eleven.

There were loads of people in the waiting room. Clowns juggling fruit, twenty girls in tutus, five women with dogs that do tricks, nine magicians pulling animals out of hats and one knife thrower with tattoos slicing an apple with a blade that he held between his gold teeth. Me and Jas found two wooden chairs in the middle of the room and waited.

The time went fast. We ran through the routine twice an hour. There were so many people to watch and so much to think about that, every time I looked at the clock, the hands seemed to have jumped forward thirty minutes. I kept imagining Dad finding the letter by his bed and rushing into the shower and choosing a smart outfit for the show. I kept imagining Mum putting on a pretty dress and saying *It's none of your business where I am going, Nigel* and buying us a Congratulations card at the petrol station on the motorway to Manchester. They'd probably see each other outside and grin and shake their heads and say *Kids* in a groany-proud way, as if they couldn't quite believe we were brave enough to organise such a great surprise. They'd choose seats near the front and share an ice cream and enjoy all the one hundred and twelve acts before us, but then we would come on and Jas would look just like Rose and Dad would be happy that she'd gone back to normal and they'd both say *Wow* when I started to dance in my Spider-Man top.

This was the first nicest thing I thought about in the waiting room. The second nicest thing involved two sparkling eyes and two brown hands clapping harder than anyone as I sang my last note and raised my arms into the air.

The one hundred and fifth act went on stage. Jas's leg started to twitch. She looked pale and young in her new clothes with her new hair and I got this strong urge to protect her. I put my arm around her shoulders, even though it was hard to reach, and she smiled and whispered *Thanks*. Her bones jutted out of her skin and I said *You should eat more*. She looked surprised. *You are thin enough* I said and her eyes filled with tears. Girls are strange. We held

141

hands and waited.

One hundred and eight. One hundred and nine. One hundred and ten. There were only two acts left before us now. The waiting room was getting empty. It smelled of sweat and face paint and old food and it was boiling 'cos the radiators were on full blast. The music started for number one hundred and eleven. The old man had only sung five notes when his CD was turned off and the judges told him that he had no talent. The audience started chanting *Off Off Off Off* and Jas went green. *I can't do this* she said, shaking her head and holding her stomach. *I really don't think I can do this. My horoscope said not to take a risk.*

The old man came through the door that led from the stage and collapsed onto a chair. He put his bald head into his hands and his shoulders shook 'cos he was crying. TV cameras had followed him off stage and were zooming right up close and he said *Get away* like he was mental when really he was just upset that his dream was over. There were sequins all over his t-shirt and sequins all over his trousers and it must have taken him days to sew them all on and he only got to go on stage for ten seconds.

I honestly can't do this Jas said, and she was watching the old man with this terrified look on her face. *My horoscope was right. This is a bad idea. I'm sorry, Jamie.* She actually stood up and started walking off. Until then I thought she was just being dramatic. *Wait* I said and my voice came out in a squeak. I was terrified that Jas was going to leave. *Please don't go.* She didn't listen. She was running now and her pigtails were bouncing and she was near the door that said EXIT. The girl with the clipboard shouted *Number one hundred and twelve* and a man dressed as Michael Jackson took a deep breath and stood up. Jas was at the door. Her fingers tightened around the handle. I couldn't let her leave. *Think about Mum* I shouted. *Think about Dad. And Leo*. She pushed open the door and icy air gushed in but Jas didn't walk out. I ran up to her and grabbed her hand. *Do you really think they're watching* she whispered, her eyes wide in her white face. *Yes* I replied. *Leo dropped us off and he promised that*—She shook her head. *Not Leo* she said, biting her lip too hard. A tiny spot of blood trickled out of a cut. She dabbed it with her finger. She'd even taken the black polish off her nails and had painted them pale pink. *Mum*.

That flicker came back again, stronger than ever before, and for the first time I knew exactly what it was. Doubt. If envy is red then doubt is black and the room went all dark and it was the opposite of the egg yolk car. Everything looked ugly and everything felt hopeless. I thought about my birthday and the P.S. and Parents' Evening but I nodded and said *She's here*.

She didn't come for Christmas Jas said in the tiniest voice I'd ever heard her use. A tear dripped down her cheek as the music for Michael Jackson's Thriller started on stage. *No* I said, my insides in a knot. *But she probably thought that she wasn't invited*. Jas looked at me with watery eyes. *I invited her* she whispered and the knot got tighter. I remembered how Jas kept glancing out of the window on Christmas Day. *I sent her a card and asked her to come and cook the turkey*. She was crying hard now and it was difficult to hear what she was saying and it was difficult to concentrate 'cos my tummy ached so badly. *And I wrote to her before that. All about Dad and how we needed help because he drinks too much and doesn't look after us properly. But she didn't come, Jamie. She's abandoned us.*

On TV, my worst advert is one called Sponsor A Dog. It shows all these different dogs that have been left by their owners in bins or boxes or by the side of lonely roads. There's always sad music playing and the dogs' tails are all droopy and their eyes are full of pain. This man with a London accent goes on and on about how they've been left, and how nobody in the world loves them enough to take care of them. And that is what abandoned means.

Mum loves us I said, but all I could hear in my head was the London accent saying *Jamie needs a new owner*, and I had to block it out. *Mum loves us Mum loves us Mum lo—* Jas shook her head and her pigtails wobbled by her ears. *She doesn't, Jamie* she replied, her voice all strangled. Tears dripped off her chin. *How can she. She walked out on us. On my BIRTHDAY.* Jas shouted this last bit 'cos I'd put my hands over my ears to shut out the words. I started singing the Michael Jackson song. I didn't want to hear any more. *My birthday* she said again, pulling my hands away from my head and closing my lips with her fingers. *And we haven't heard from her since.* I struggled free. *You're lying* I yelled, stamping my foot, suddenly angry. The knife thrower looked at us and shook his head but I didn't care. My blood was on fire and it burned through my body and I wanted to kick and thump and scream and shout and let it all out in a massive volcano. *That's not true. Mum sent me a present and it was the best present I ever got and I love it and*

144

YOU'RE LYING.

The music for Thriller stopped.

Number one hundred and thirteen.

Jas opened her mouth to say something. I waited, panting, but then she shook her head as if changing her mind. *Fine. Mum sent you a birthday present. Big deal*.

Number one hundred and thirteen the girl with the clipboard said again, sounding fed up. She looked from an old lady in tap shoes, to a little boy with a parrot, to me and Jas. *Where are you. One one three can you come forward now.*

Jas wiped her eyes and stared down at her outfit. *Look at me* she said quietly, smoothing down her flowery dress. *Look at you.* I touched the safety pins on the sleeve of my t-shirt. *Look at what we've done for them. And for what, Jamie. Mum won't have left Nigel to come up here* Jas said and she put her hand on my head and it felt safe and I stopped panting and tried to calm down. *And Dad'll be too drunk to get out of bed. It's a waste of time.* I put my hand on top of hers. *But it might not be* I said and I swallowed all the doubt and all the disappointment and all the anger and they were almost too big, like vitamin pills that are difficult to get down even with water. *Please, Jas. Please. Just in case they're watching. I don't want to give up on them.* Jas closed her eyes as if she was thinking.

Number one hundred and thirteen the girl shouted, tapping a pen on the clipboard. *You are running out of time. The judges are waiting and if you don't come, like, right NOW then you will miss your chance.*

I touched Jas's arm. *Please.* She opened her eyes and stared at me then shook her head. *It's a waste of*

145

time, Jamie. They're not here. I can't stand to see you disappointed. Not again.

Number one hundred and thirteen. The girl looked around the room one last time and then drew a big cross on the clipboard. *Fine. Let's have number one hundred and fourteen instead.*

19

My legs gave way and I crashed to the floor. My head sank into my hands. The taps on the feet of the old lady echoed through the waiting room as she walked towards the stage door.

WAIT Jas yelled and my heart stopped beating. *WAIT. We're one hundred and thirteen. We're here.*

I looked up and Jas offered me her hand. I grabbed it and she pulled me to my feet. *I'm doing this for you* she whispered and the corners of my mouth almost touched my earlobes as I grinned my biggest grin ever. *Not for Mum. Not for Dad. Not for Rose. You. Us.* I nodded and we ran forward and my heart started with a THUMP that shook my ribs. The girl with the clipboard sighed impatiently. *I shouldn't let you go on* she snapped but she opened the stage door and we sprinted up the stairs and all of a sudden there were lights and cameras and hundreds of eyes shining in the darkness of the theatre.

We walked onto the stage. The audience went quiet. I recognised one of the two judges from TV. He rolled his eyes when he saw my top. *And you are* he said. I didn't know if the right answer was Spider-Man, or James Aaron Matthews, or just

146

Jamie, so I said all three. The audience did one of those sniggers and I wondered if Mum and Dad and Sunya had joined in. Jas squeezed my fingers. They were all sticky with sweat. *And who are you* the man said and my sister replied *Jasmine Rebecca Matthews*, and he said *Not Supergirl or Catwoman* in this dead sarcastic way. Jas's arm started to shake. I wanted to kick the judge for scaring her.

What are you going to do for us today the lady judge asked. I whispered *A song and a dance*. The man yawned. *How original* he said and hundreds of people laughed and the lady hit him on the wrist and said *Behave* but then she giggled too. I tried to smile as if I was in on the joke but my teeth were too dry and my top lip got stuck. *What are you going to sing* the lady said when everything went quiet. Jas whispered *The Courage To Fly*. Both of the judges groaned and the man banged his head on the desk and the audience exploded with laughter all over again. I looked up at Jas. She was trying to be brave but I could see tears in her eyes and I felt bad 'cos she was taking this risk for me and it wasn't paying off. I half expected Dad to defend us or Mum to run onto the stage and say *Don't you dare do that to my kids*. But nothing happened.

The man said *Get on with it then* like we were boring him and all of a sudden I didn't want to do the dance and I didn't want to do the song. They felt too precious to perform in front of people who didn't understand. It was hot under the lights and the Spider-Man top stuck to my body. It felt bigger than ever, or I felt smaller than ever, and I knew that it didn't look good. Mum would be disappointed and I felt guilty, as if I was letting her down.

147

We didn't have a CD and no one counted us in so we didn't know when to start. We just sort of stood there. Everyone was waiting. A few people booed. I didn't want Mum or Dad to hear them but I didn't dare sing. The audience started chanting *Off Off Off Off* and Jas's whole body was shaking now, not just her arm. This wasn't what was supposed to happen. It was all going wrong and I didn't know how to fix it.

Off Off Off Off.

Panic rose inside my chest like one of those waves at the beach that suddenly crashes down and drenches everything. *Get these two off* the man shouted suddenly, waving his hand as if he was flicking away a fly. *They're a waste of time.*

NO. Jas said this loudly, more of a shout than anything, and the audience fell silent. *NO.* The judges looked at Jas in surprise. She stared back all brave and brilliant and the tears were gone and the shakes had vanished and suddenly she was my sister on the swing, smiling at the sky as if nothing in the world could frighten her. And 'cos she wasn't scared, I wasn't scared. And then we started to sing.

> *Your smile lifts my soul into the sky. Your strength gives me the courage to fly.*
> *A kite, I soar so grounded yet free. Your love brings out the be—*

We got further than the old man. Maybe fifteen or sixteen notes in. I didn't hear the judge say *Stop* 'cos I was running round the back of the stage flapping my wings like a fairy, or a bird, or whatever is supposed to be flying in the song. When I realised that Jas had stopped singing, my arms

148

flopped to my side and the walk back to the front of the stage felt longer than a marathon, which Mrs Farmer says is twenty six point two miles and not very good for your knee joints.

I have never been so impressed and so disgusted at the same time the man said. *That was brilliant and awful. Fantastic and terrible.* I had no idea what he was going on about and I wasn't really listening 'cos I was looking at the audience to see if I could spot Mum. *You were the awful part* the man said, pointing at me. *I mean, was that supposed to be dancing.* It was a question but it didn't seem to need an answer so I just shrugged. The man did one of those smirks and folded his arms and the audience laughed. *But you* he went on, pointing at Jas. *You were the brilliant part. That was absolutely magnificent. Where did you learn to sing like that.* Jas looked surprised and said *Mum taught me when I was little but I haven't sung for five years.* The man whispered something behind his hand to the lady. The cameras zoomed in on them and then on us. The audience held its breath. *Yes, yes, I agree* the lady said and the man turned to us with a smile. *We'd like you to try again* he said and Jas nodded and I got ready to flutter my arms and sing the first note. *Without the dance moves. Without your brother.*

Jas looked at me as if she didn't know what to do, but I raised my thumb. It was better for her to go through than us both to go out. And I know she's better than me so it wasn't really a shock. I can sing okay but she's the one with the voice of an angel. I hoped Dad was paying attention.

The man pointed to some steps at the side of the stage that led into the audience. I walked over to them and sat down as Jas took a deep breath. The lights on the stage disappeared, all except one. It dazzled Jas and made her blink. The man folded his arms and leaned back in his chair. The lady put her chin on her hand. Jas walked forward and the spotlight followed. *When you're ready* the man said and Jas began. Quiet at first. Shaky. But after a couple of lines her shoulders relaxed and her mouth widened and the sound was beautiful. It flew into the air like that kite at St. Bees.

Jas sang with every bit of her body. She sang with her eyes and her hands and her heart and when she hit the top note the audience was on their feet and the judges were clapping and everyone was cheering but no one as loudly as me. I forgot where I was. I forgot I was on stage in front of hundreds of people and maybe Mum and maybe Dad and loads of TV cameras. I forgot everything but my sister and the words of her song. They made sense for the first time and gave me a brave feeling like that lion in the sky was somewhere in my chest.

The song finished. Jas took a little bow as the whole theatre roared. The judges pointed at me and then at the middle of the stage. I stood up and I felt like a different boy and I hoped Mum would notice how my shoulders pushed back and how my chest puffed out as if it was a big bagpipe that a Scottish man had blown pride into.

Well, it was a rubbish song the man started. The audience booed but this time they were on our side. *A really horrible choice.* I grinned and Jas grinned. We didn't care what the judges thought. Not any more. *The dance was appalling* the man went on. *And young Spider-Man here, well, you might be a superhero but you certainly can't sing.* Jas put her hand on my shoulder. *But you, young lady. Let's just say*—he paused dramatically and looked Jas right in the eye—*that was the best audition I have seen today*. The audience clapped. *We'll see you in the next round*. The audience cheered. *Without your brother, of course*. The audience laughed. *Next* the man shouted and it was time to leave. I started walking off the stage.

You won't Jas said and I stopped and spun round and the judges raised their eyebrows. *We won't what* the man said. Jas's voice was loud and clear as she replied *You won't see me in the next round*. The audience gasped. The man looked shocked. *Don't be ridiculous* he said. *This is a chance of a lifetime. This competition could change your life*. Jas grabbed my hand and squeezed. *What if we don't want it to change* she said and then she looked, not at the judges, but out into the audience. She raised her voice and I knew who she was talking to. *I won't audition without Jamie. I won't abandon my brother. Families should stick together.*

*   *   *

We walked off the stage to the sound of cheers that went on for ages. The girl with the clipboard shook her head but all the other acts gathered round. They said *That was brilliant* and *Congratulations* and, even though it was mostly for Jas, I reckon a little bit was for me and it felt good. I offered my hand to our fans and shook every single one like Leo or Wayne Rooney and my t-shirt seemed to fit and I felt grown up. Maybe it was different to be in double figures after all. Then we sat down and waited for the show to finish and we didn't speak 'cos our happiness was too big for words.

Let's find Leo Jas said an hour later when the final act, a man who sang opera while standing on his head, had finished. We walked out of the waiting room. It was dark outside and snow was still falling. We walked into the main entrance and there were these big sparkly lights all posh on the ceiling that looked like huge dangly earrings. The carpet was red and the banisters were gold and the theatre smelled of sweets and success. I was searching for Sunya and searching for Dad and searching searching searching for Mum, a smile the size of a new moon on my face.

We pushed our way through the crowd and everyone was looking and nodding and smiling 'cos they recognised us from the stage. One man put his hand into the air to do a high five but I missed. And an old lady croaked *You made me cry* and I said *Shut up* but Jas said *Thanks* so it must have been a compliment, even though it sounded mean. Jas was looking for spiky green and I was looking for sparkly brown and our necks were long and our eyes were darting and our feet were striding and our heads were twisting and then we

STOPPED. We saw them at exactly the same moment. Twenty metres away. Two faces, staring in opposite directions. Silent. Like strangers. Not Leo. Not Sunya. Mum and Dad.

Mum!

I shouted it as loud as I could but she didn't hear.

Mum!!

Too many people swarmed around the theatre

152

entrance. I was pushed to the side by a man in clown make-up. *You were wonderful* squealed his wife, kissing his bright red nose. Standing on tiptoes, I tried to see Mum over the top of their heads.

Black boots.

Blue jeans.

Green coat.

And hands.

Pink, living, real hands that clutched a black bag, fiddling with the silver zip. Hands that had cooked dinner and rubbed headaches and had shoved jumpers over my head on cold days. Hands that had tucked me in bed. Hands that had taught me to draw.

Bloody hell Jas said. *She actually came.* We stood still and stared, the theatre buzzing around us.

Mum was tanned. Her eyes were surrounded by all these wrinkles I hadn't seen before. And she'd cut off her hair. There were a few grey bits near her temples and some blonde streaks on top. She looked different. But she was here. I brushed down my t-shirt and straightened the collar and sorted out the sleeves, never taking my eyes off Mum in case she disappeared.

Suddenly she spotted us. Jas swore. I waved and Mum went red and lifted her arm but didn't move her hand. It fell to her side. She said something to Dad, who ignored her. *Here goes* Jas whispered, putting an arm around me. I could feel her ribs go up and down as we pushed through the crowd.

Time went too slow and too fast, all at the same time, and then we were standing in front of Mum and the air crackled like Rice Krispies 'cos hundreds of feelings popped and snapped in the space between us. I waited for her to give me a hug, or to kiss the top of my head, or to notice my Spider-Man top, but she just smiled then stared at the floor.

Hi I said. *Hi* Mum replied. *Hi* muttered Jas. I leaned forward and opened my arms. Mum didn't move. I'd gone too far to pull out of the hug. I had to go for it. I moved towards Mum and wrapped my arms around hers, shocked to find I almost came up to her shoulder when I used to be the same height as her chest. *She's shrunk* I thought, which was stupid, but that was how it felt. We had contact for less than two seconds. I wanted the hug to be perfect, but it was cold and hard and made me think of jigsaw pieces that don't fit together, no matter how hard you push.

Your song was great Mum said when she pulled away. Her words sounded empty, as if they were written with a very thin pencil on a big piece of paper and there was too much space inside all the letters. *You're so talented.* I said *Thanks* as Mum said *What a voice.* She'd been talking to Jas, not me, and I blushed.

Silence.

I wanted to tell Mum about my goal and the tricks at Halloween and the black chicken in Dad's roast dinner. I wanted to tell her about Mrs Farmer and the dicks in Daniel's stable and how I'd met a friend who was the best girl on the planet, apart from my sister. If Mum had asked me, or even

154

looked in my direction, it would have come blurting out. But she just stared at the floor.

Let's get out of here Dad said at last. As we walked out of the theatre, he did something he's not done before. He put his hand on my shoulder and squeezed.

The pavement was icy and the snowflakes looked orange as they fluttered past the streetlights. Someone beeped their horn and Leo sped past, green hair behind a black steering wheel, zooming down the road. *Who's that* Mum asked, and Jas shrugged. It was too hard to explain. Mum had missed too much. But she'd catch up. I'd help her. We had all the time in the world.

Dad got the car keys out of his pocket. He rattled them in his hand. *Ready* he asked Jas. She nodded. *Jamie* he said, and I grinned. This was the bit I'd been looking forward to.

I was just wondering if Mum would ring Nigel and tell him it was over and call him a bastard, when she said *I guess I'll see you all soon*. I thought she meant *Back at the cottage* 'cos she had to drive so I said *I'll come with you*. Jas's shoulders shot up to her ears as if she'd just seen a dog run into the road and she couldn't do a thing to stop it getting hurt. Dad went pale and closed his eyes. Mum rubbed her nose. I didn't understand why everyone was acting strange. *I'll show you the way* I said and she asked *Back to London* and then I understood.

Only joking I said and I forced myself to laugh but every *ha* burned my throat. Mum got some gloves out of her bag and put them on her pink hands. *Well, bye then* she said. *It was lovely to see you. You're all doing so well*. Dad snorted. Mum winced. A bus drove through slush and drenched

155

Jas's bare legs.

Here Mum said, pulling a tissue out of her bag. She gave it to Jas, who looked at it blankly. *Dry your legs* Mum said, her voice suddenly back to normal. Impatient. A bit snappy. It was the best noise in the world. Jas did as she was told. *You look beautiful* Mum said as Jas rubbed her shins. I pushed out my chest so the red and blue material was right under Mum's nose. She didn't even glance at it. *So like your sister.*

Let's go Dad said quickly. *The snow's sticking.* Mum nodded. *See you soon* she lied, touching Jas's shoulder and patting my head. *And well done.*

Mum walked off, black boots splashing, green coat swishing. I didn't recognise her clothes. They were new. I wondered when she'd bought them. On my birthday. Or the afternoon of the football match. Or maybe Parents' Evening.

And then all of a sudden I was chasing after her, dodging past dancers and singers and hundreds of happy faces, all red in the cold. *MUM* I yelled at the top of my voice. *MUM.* She turned around. *What is it, sweetheart* she asked and I wanted to shout *DON'T CALL ME THAT* but I had more important things to say.

We were standing outside an Italian restaurant and I could smell pizza and I should have been hungry but my tummy hurt too much for food. I could hear people laughing and waiters talking and glasses clinking like they do when you say *Cheers*. The restaurant glowed with candles and I wished I was in there, away from the cold grey street.

What is it Mum said again. I didn't want to ask the question. I was scared of the answer. But I thought of Jas and the words of the chorus and I

156

forced myself to be brave. *Are you working tomorrow* I panted. Mum looked confused. She pulled her coat around her. *Why* she said, as if she was worried that I was going to ask her to stay longer. *Just want to know* I breathed. She shook her head. *No. I stopped teaching months ago.*

Everything started to spin. I thought of a globe on a metal holder, a hand whirling it round and round. *So you don't work for Mr Walker* I asked, giving her a chance to change her answer, hating the way my heart pounded in my chest with the very last bit of hope. Mum shook her head again. *No* she said. *I don't have a job. I've been away. Travelling. Nigel had to do some research for his book in Egypt and I went with him. I only got back on New Year's Eve.* Well, that explained the tan.

Mum opened her bag one more time. She took out four envelopes, two with my writing on the front, two with Jas's. *I didn't get them in time* she said quietly, as if she was apologising, as if she wanted me to say it was okay to miss Parents' Evening, and fine to miss Christmas. *I would've come* she said. I don't know if she was telling the truth.

I had one more question and this one was even more difficult to ask. The world spun faster, cars and people and buildings a dizzy blur round me and Mum. *The t-shirt* I began, my eyes on a puddle on the pavement. *Oh yes* Mum said. *I meant to say.* She smiled. *It's brilliant.* And I smiled back, despite everything. She rubbed the material between her thumb and finger. *It's a lovely top. Where did you get it from. It really does suit you, James.*

20

I didn't even speak when we got back to the cottage and Dad asked if I wanted a hot chocolate. For some reason I'd spent the whole journey thinking about earthquakes and, as I walked into the hall, all I could see was the ground shaking and buildings falling in some far away place like China. I wondered if they had earthquakes in Bangladesh and if Sunya would tell me about them at school. She didn't come to the talent show even though I invited her in the Christmas card and covered the *Please* in gold glitter. She must still be cross with me so she won't want to talk about natural disasters any time soon. *Do you want a hot chocolate* Jas said softly. I just nodded and went upstairs to find Roger. He wasn't in my room. I sat down on the windowsill and stared at my reflection in the glass. The Spider-Man t-shirt looked rubbish.

Maybe Mum had been joking. Or maybe she had forgotten that she sent it.

Yes. That had to be it. I nodded and my reflection nodded back.

She had forgotten.

Mum always forgets stuff. She goes to supermarkets and can't remember what she wants to buy. And she can never find her keys 'cos she forgets where she puts them. Once they turned up in the freezer underneath a bag of frozen peas and she had no idea how they got there. No wonder she can't remember something that happened one hundred and thirty two days ago.

Dad walked in with my hot chocolate. Steam

swirled out of the blue cup. *Here you go* he said, sitting on my bed. Since we moved into the cottage, Dad's only been in my bedroom once and that was when he was drunk and looking for the toilet.

I didn't know what to say so I sipped my drink even though it was too hot and burned my tongue. *Nice* he asked, nodding at the cup. It wasn't, but I said *Mmmm* anyway. He hadn't stirred the chocolate powder in properly. It was all at the bottom of the cup like mud. But it was hot and it was sweet and Dad had made it so it was good. He looked all pleased with himself as he watched me drink. *Good for the bones. Grow up to be strong like Rooney if you drink one of them a day* he said. *I'll make them for you.* He was going red and rubbing his hand over his chin and it made a nice noise 'cos of the whiskers. I said *Okay* and, as he stood up, he squeezed my shoulder for the second time that day.

I'm going to the building site on Monday morning he said suddenly, staring at his foot as it moved back and forward and back and forward over the glitter on the carpet. *If they'll still have me. It'll do me good. Something to get up for.* He cleared his throat even though there was nothing in it. *Something to stay sober for.*

When I spray my deodorant, all the tiny drops hang in the air for ages and don't disappear. That's exactly what the word *Sober* did. It just stayed there and I couldn't look up 'cos I didn't want to see it swirling around Dad. I stared at the powder in the bottom of my cup as if it was the most interesting thing I had ever seen. It was dark brown almost black and drying in funny shapes. Jas reads her horoscope and some people read palms and some people read tea-leaves to tell their fortune. I squinted at the chocolate powder blobs but they didn't reveal anything about my future. *Finished* Dad said and I said *Yeah.* He took my cup and walked out of my room.

I couldn't sleep. I lay in bed with a tummy ache and I rolled on my right side and then on my back and then on my left side and then on my front but I couldn't get comfy. My bed was too hot and I turned my pillow over to find some cool. I kept saying *She forgot that she sent it she forgot that she sent it* but the doubt had come back and everything was black and I didn't believe the words in my head.

Mum gave up her job months ago. Mum doesn't work for Mr Walker or any other mean boss. Mum didn't have to teach when I invited her to Parents' Evening. And she wasn't even in the country when Jas invited her for Christmas.

She'd been in Egypt with Nigel while we'd been sitting in the cottage, waiting.

But she was at the theatre. She drove all the way from London to Manchester to see us in the show. That had to mean something.

I felt all wobbly and dizzy. I didn't know what to believe. All the facts that were strong and safe and big and true had come crashing down. Like buildings in an earthquake. They don't just happen in China or Bangladesh. There was one in my bedroom and it was shaking things up and smashing stuff to the ground and changing my life forever.

Granny says *Be careful what you wish for because it might come true* and I always thought it was stupid. Until now. *Ring this number to change your life*. I wished I'd never picked up the phone.

*   *   *

160

When I opened my eyes, sunlight was pouring through the window. I blinked twelve times to get used to the light. I yawned and it hurt my head and my eyes felt bruised. I hadn't slept very well. I got out of bed and I expected Roger to rub his fur against my shins and wrap his tail around my ankles, but he wasn't there. I hadn't seen him since I got back from the contest. I stared out of the window. The garden was almost too bright to look at with the sun reflecting off the snow. I could just about see the tree and the pond and the bushes. But no Roger.

I ran to the kitchen. I looked at Roger's bowl. His food was still there. Not eaten. I raced into the lounge. I looked behind the sofa. I searched behind the chairs. I sprinted up the stairs. Strange chemical smells were drifting under Jas's door. I turned the handle and walked in. *Get out of my room* she yelled. *I'm naked.* Probably a lie but I shut my eyes. *Have you seen Roger* I asked. *Not since yesterday morning* she replied. *You shut him out of the lounge when we were practising the routine.* If guilt was an animal then it would be an octopus. All slimy and wriggly with hundreds of arms that wrap around your insides and squeeze them tight.

I went into Dad's room. He was asleep on his back with his mouth wide open, snoring loudly. I shook him. *What* he groaned, covering his face with his arm and licking his dry lips. They were covered in brown stuff that looked like hot chocolate and he didn't smell too strongly of alcohol. *Have you seen Roger* I asked and Dad said *I let him out yesterday before I drove to Manchester* and then he fell back to sleep.

161

I pulled on my wellies, put on a coat and set off.

I searched the back garden. I shouted Roger's name. Nothing happened. I squeaked like a mouse and I squealed like a rabbit to try and make him stop sulking and start hunting. He didn't come out of his hiding place. I looked up the tree to make sure he wasn't stuck on a branch and I searched for paw prints but the snow was fresh and there weren't any marks. The pond had melted and my fish was swimming and I said *Hello again* before I left the garden.

Roger isn't a moody cat so I was surprised he was being so grumpy. I walked down the road and my head felt hot 'cos of the sun but my feet felt cold 'cos of the snow. Every time something moved, I expected to see Roger's orange face. First it was a bird and then it was a sheep and then it was a grey dog running down the path with a red Christmas bow tied around its neck. I patted him and said *Nice dog* to the owner. *He's a bit too energetic for me, lad* said the old man, who was smoking a pipe and had a flat cap on his head. His hair was the exact same colour as the dog's fur and he had a kind face and brown eyes with heavy lids that made him look sleepy. *Have you seen a cat* I asked. *A ginger one* the man frowned. *Yeah* I replied, laughing 'cos the dog jumped up and put his icy paws on my tummy. *Down, Fred* the man muttered. Fred wagged his tail and ignored him. *A ginger cat* the man said again, and I didn't understand why he had gone pale or why his hand shook when he pointed down the road. *Over there.*

Thanks I said with relief. I pushed Fred down. He licked my hands and wagged his whole body. *I'm sorry* the old man said, his voice all wobbly. *I'm so sorry.*

And that's when I knew.

That's when I knew that Roger wasn't hiding. That's when I knew he wasn't just in a mood. I shook my head. *No* I said. *No.* The old man chewed the end of his pipe. *I'm so sorry, lad. I think your cat—*

NO I roared, pushing the old man out of my way. *NO.* I ran down the road, scared of what I might see but desperate to find Roger to show the old man that he was wrong, that Roger was okay, that my cat was just—

Oh.

In all the white snow there was a bright orange blob. Tiny. Lying on the road. Fifty metres away. *It's not him* I said to myself but my blood froze like that witch in Narnia had made it winter but not Christmas. The sun shone on my head but I could not feel it. I didn't want to walk another step but my feet weren't listening to my brain and they were moving fast, too fast, down the road. It could be a fox. Thirty metres away. Please let it be a fox. Twenty metres. It was a cat. Ten metres. And it was covered in blood.

I stared at Roger. His glittery tail twinkled in the sunlight. I waited for him to move. Waited for five whole minutes for him, something, anything to move. But Roger was still. His legs looked too stiff and his ears looked too sharp and his eyes were glassy green marbles.

I hate dead things. They scare me. Roger's mouse. Roger's rabbit. Roger. I took a deep breath. It didn't help. The octopus was holding my lungs and squeezing them hard. There wasn't enough air. There would never be enough air. I started to pant.

163

I thought about the last time I saw Roger. He purred in my arms but I dropped him on the hall carpet. I closed the door in his face when he just wanted a stroke. I ignored his meows at the door and I didn't even say goodbye when I went to the audition. I didn't say goodbye. And now it was too late.

The snow underneath Roger was red. A sudden gust of wind blew his fur and he looked cold so I tiptoed forward. My teeth rattled in my head. My shoulders moved up and down as I tried to suck air into my chest. I was only two metres away now. I dropped to my knees and crawled closer. Slowly. Slowly. My heart bashed against my ribs.

Roger's side was cut open. It looked deep and gooey. His front legs were twisted at a funny angle. Broken. Snapped. I thought about Roger sneaking off into the bushes and Roger running through the garden and Roger jumping out of my arms and landing on strong legs that still worked. I couldn't stand the thought of him all cracked and cut and cold. I had to fix him.

I pushed out my finger. I moved my arm forward. My fingertip brushed his fur but my hand flew back as if it had just touched something hot. I was panting so hard I felt faint. I tried again. And again and again and again. I thought about the rabbit I lifted up with sticks and the mouse I carried on paper and, for some reason, Rose. Rose blown into bits. My throat burned painfully. I tried to swallow but the spit wouldn't go down.

On the sixth try, I touched him. My arm was shaking and my palm was sweating but I put my hand on Roger's back and held it there. He felt different. I remembered all the times I'd put my

164

fingers in his fur, feeling warm skin and beating heart and ribs vibrating with a purr. They were still, now. There was no life left in his whiskers. No life left in his eyes. No life left in his tail. I wondered where it had all gone.

The burn in my throat spread to my cheeks. They went from freezing cold to boiling hot in less than a millisecond. I stroked Roger's head. Told him I loved him. Said I was sorry. He didn't meow. I saw some tyre marks in the snow. Deep and short and diagonal, where someone had put the brakes on quickly and skidded on the road.

All the hurt turned into anger. With a shout of rage I jumped up and kicked the tyre marks. I stamped on them. Spat on them. Grabbed the snow in my hot fingers and threw it into the sky. I fell to my knees and punched the tyre marks as hard as I could and my fist hit the road and the pain felt good. The skin on my knuckles split open. I hit the road again.

If I hadn't gone to the talent contest, Roger would still be alive. Last night I'd have noticed that he wasn't in the cottage and I'd have gone to look for him and he would have come running up and he would have rubbed his body on my wellies and his fur would have glinted in the moonlight. But I'd been too busy worrying about Mum to worry about Roger.

I stopped thumping the ground. I stood up and my knees shook. I walked over to Roger and this time I didn't feel scared of his dead body. I wanted to hold him. I never wanted to let him go. I wanted to give him a thousand strokes. A million cuddles. Say all the things I should have said when he could still hear my voice. I picked him up gently as if he was one of those boxes marked SACRED. His head flopped on his neck but I lifted it onto my shoulder. I pulled his body close to mine and stroked his fur. I rubbed his head and rocked him gently, like women do with babies.

I missed my cat. I missed him so much that the burn in my throat and the burn in my cheeks spread up to my eyes and burned them too. They started to water. No. Not water. Cry.

I cried. For the first time in five years. And my silver tears fell into Roger's orange fur.

21

I hated how cold he was. Roger had been outside too long. I unzipped my jacket and pulled him against my Spider-Man top. Then I zipped it up again to shelter him from the breeze and the snow that had started to fall. His head poked out of the top of my jacket and I kissed it gently. His whiskers tickled my lips.

I carried him home. I walked around all the icy bits on the road so that I wouldn't slip. I couldn't see the cottage through my tears but I walked up the drive and straight into the back garden. I was talking to Roger all the time now, telling him about the audition, how amazing Jas had been, how I'd understood the words of the song for the very first time and how they might have changed me. I told him I'd wanted to make Mum proud and that was why, that was why I'd shut him out of the lounge. I explained that I closed the door 'cos I was practising, and I wanted to impress Mum 'cos I was

166

stupid, and I hadn't realised it was pointless until it was too late. I whispered *Mum's a liar and she abandoned me and nothing I can do will ever make her love me.* I wanted Roger to purr or meow so I knew that he forgave me. But he was silent.

I didn't know what to do with my cat when I reached the pond. I didn't want to bury him. I thought about his body under the ground, rotting away, and I was almost sick. I cuddled him hard, desperate to keep him just as he was, tight against my chest, bleeding all over my t-shirt.

But I knew I had to do something. Roger deserved a proper funeral. I thought about my sister on the mantelpiece. It would be nice to have my cat there too. I pictured an orange urn with Roger's ashes inside. Then I could still talk to him and stroke him and hug him whenever I wanted. And all of a sudden I understood. All of a sudden I got it. Why Rose was in the urn on the mantelpiece. Why Dad found it too hard to sprinkle her in the sea. Why he gave her cake on birthdays, and why he fastened her seatbelt, and why he hung a stocking by the urn on Christmas Eve. It was too hard to let go. He loved her too much to say goodbye.

I fell to my knees and put my face in Roger's fur and cried until I couldn't breathe. My nose was running and my head was thumping and my face was swollen but I couldn't stop. I heard a window open behind me. I heard Dad shout *Jamie, get inside. It's freezing out there.* I didn't move.

If I couldn't have Roger, I wanted his ashes. I found two twigs and held one between my feet and used my right hand to rub the other against it. I cuddled Roger with my left arm and sang into his ear so he wouldn't hear the sticks rub together and get scared. It didn't work though. It was too wet for the twigs to catch fire.

I heard the back door open and I turned around. Dad. *It's freezing* he said again, but then he stopped. *Roger.*

Dad pulled me to my feet and gave me the first hug that I can remember. It was strong and tight and safe and I pushed my face into his chest. My shoulders shook and my breath came in gasps and my tears made his t-shirt wet. He didn't tell me to *Sssh* and he didn't say *Calm down* and he didn't ask *What's wrong*. He knew it hurt too much to say out loud.

When there were no more tears left, Dad patted me on the back and unzipped my jacket. I didn't stop him. He took Roger off me, gently slowly softly, and lowered him to the ground. He touched Roger's eyelids and closed them carefully. The marbles disappeared. Roger looked like he was fast asleep.

Wait there he said. His eyes were sad but his mouth was determined. He disappeared inside the cottage. A minute later, he was back, carrying a spade and a small object that he dropped into his pocket. I started to say *Cremate him* but Dad said *We can't build a fire in the snow*. I tried to pick Roger up, to take him away. I didn't want my cat to be buried underground. Dad grabbed my arm and said *He's gone*. He nodded his head, convincing himself of something. His eyes filled with tears but he took a deep breath and blinked them away. He nodded again as if he'd made a big decision. Started to dig. Said *Whatever was there has disappeared*. His voice was tight with a sadness I thought I understood.

168

It took a long time. The ground was hard. All the time Dad worked, I stroked Roger's head, telling him again and again that I loved him. More tears filled my eyes and trickled down my face. I didn't want the hole to get deep enough. I didn't want Dad to finish. I wasn't ready to say goodbye. Jas appeared at some point. I didn't hear her. One minute she wasn't there and the next she was crouched by my side, crying quietly, stroking Roger's bloody fur. Her hair was bright pink again. She'd dyed it back.

Dad stopped too quickly. *It's done* he said. *You ready.* I shook my head. *We'll do it together* Dad whispered and he took the small object from his pocket. The golden urn. *We'll do it together.*

Sometimes Mrs Farmer said it's too cold for rain and that's how Dad's face looked. Too sad for tears. He walked over to the pond. Jas stood up and crossed her arms, hugging her own body. I lifted Roger. Dad opened the urn. The sun shone stronger than it had done all day. Light bounced off the gold urn, making it sparkle.

I walked to the hole. Dad emptied some of Rose into his hand. No. Not Rose. Rose had gone. Dad emptied some of the ashes into his hand. I put Roger into the grave. Dad took a deep breath. I took a deeper one. Everything was still for a few seconds. A bird sang and a breeze shook the bare trees. Dad let go of the ashes. He didn't say goodbye. He didn't need to this time. Rose left a long time ago.

The first ashes fluttered down to the pond, mixing with the snow that fell from the sky. They landed on top of the water and sank. I could see my fish swimming near the lily pad. I grabbed the spade and scooped up some mud. My hands were sweaty on the metal handle. I held the spade over the hole but I couldn't turn it. I couldn't drop the mud on top of my cat. *Roger's gone* I told myself. *He's gone. That's not him. Whatever was there has disappeared.* It didn't help one bit. All I could see was Roger's black nose and Roger's silver whiskers and Roger's long tail and I wanted to get him out of the grave. I wasn't ready for him to be dead yet.

Dad tipped the urn again. More ashes fell onto his palm. He clenched his teeth and turned over his hand. Rose's ashes dropped into the pond. If Dad could do it, so could I. I tipped the mud into the grave.

I couldn't look at Roger. I couldn't watch his body disappear under dirt. I whispered *I love you* and *You'll always be my best pet* and *I will miss you* and then I pushed mud into the grave as quickly as possible. I didn't wait to see what Dad was doing. I knew that if I stopped even for one millisecond then I wouldn't be able to carry on.

I patted down the top of the grave to make it all neat and flat. Then I dropped the spade as if it had germs or something. I couldn't believe what I had done. I felt sick at myself, sick at the world, sick in my tummy and my heart and my head. Jas put her arm around my shoulder and held me as I cried. Roger was gone. I'd never see him again. This was too scary to think about so I rubbed the tears out of my eyes and forced myself to stare at Dad. He was still by the pond, still sprinkling Rose's ashes into the water. Bit by bit.

I walked over to him, pulling Jas by the hand. We stood either side of Dad and watched the ashes fall. My fish was swimming in a pretty pattern, his tail wiggling happily, and some of the ashes landed on his golden skin and stuck to his shiny scales.

There was only one handful of ashes left now. The last few specks fell onto Dad's palm. He lifted the urn and looked right into it, shocked there was nothing left. His hands shook.

Don't I said suddenly. *Don't do it.* Dad's fingers curled around the last few ashes. *What* he said, breathing heavily, his face whiter than the snow all around us. *Don't do it* I repeated. *Keep those.* Dad shook his head. *Rose has gone* he said with difficulty. He held the ashes up. *These aren't her.* I stopped crying. *I know* I said. *But they were. They were part of her body. You should keep them. Just a few.* Dad looked at me and I looked back and something big zoomed between our eyes. He dropped the last few ashes inside the golden urn.

We were freezing so we went indoors. Dad disappeared upstairs for two minutes and Jas made three cups of tea. We didn't speak as we drank them in the lounge. The mantelpiece looked empty without the urn. I realised Dad must have put it in his bedroom. Out of sight. But there if he needs it, which he will on the really sad days like September 9th. I know I'll never forget that Roger died on January 6th for as long as I live, even if I have a billion pets, 'cos none of them will ever be as good as my cat.

When we finished our tea we just sort of stared at each other. Something big had happened to us that morning. Everything was different. And even though my tummy ached and my heart ached and my throat ached and the tears kept falling, I knew that the change wasn't all bad. That something good had happened too.

Jas still didn't eat. Dad still drank. But we stayed together all day. In the lounge. Not really speaking but not wanting to go to our bedrooms either. We watched a film. Jas asked me if I wanted to watch Spider-Man but I said *No* so she put on a comedy instead. We didn't laugh, but we smiled at the best bits. And Dad told Jas *I like your hair* and when she said *Thanks* he replied *You should keep it pink*. And when it was time to go to bed and the stars shone in the sky like hundreds of cats' eyes on a dark road, Dad gave me my second hug ever. It was as strong and tight and safe as the first. And as I lay under my duvet, missing Roger, wishing he was on my windowsill instead of lying underground, Dad came into my room with a hot chocolate. He put it in my hands and the steam felt nice on my face. This time the powder had been stirred right in.

22

School started again the next day. I kept expecting Roger to rub his body against my shins when I got out of bed, or jump onto my lap while I ate my Coco Pops, or twist his tail around my ankles as I brushed my teeth. The cottage felt empty without him. I felt empty without him.

Dad got out of bed in time to take us to school. He was a bit hung-over but it didn't matter one bit. Dad's not perfect. And neither am I. He's trying, and that means everything. He hasn't always done a good job but he's done a million times better than Mum. He hasn't abandoned us. He's just sad about Rose and that's fine. Having a cat killed is bad enough. Having a daughter blown to bits must be horrid.

When we pulled up outside school, Dad saw Sunya on the pavement. I could see his face in the mirror. He clenched his jaw but he didn't shout *Muslims killed my daughter* or anything like that. He didn't even tell me to keep away from her. He just said that he wouldn't be home until six 'cos of work. Jas squeezed his arm and Dad smiled in a proud way and then he said *Have a good day. You got an excellent report so keep it up*.

I walked into school. I was still wearing the Spider-Man t-shirt, but not for Mum 'cos she didn't send it. Roger's blood had soaked into the material so I didn't want to take it off. I know I must have looked like a murderer or something but I didn't care. I wanted to be close to my cat.

Here comes sissy boy shouted Daniel down the corridor. He was standing outside the classroom with Ryan. I was scared but I didn't go red or start shaking or run off. I walked towards them. *Sissy boy in his sad Spider-Man t-shirt*. They sniggered and did a high five in the air. I walked right underneath it. Daniel kicked me on the back of the leg and it hurt and I wanted to punch him in the face, but I didn't want to get beaten up again. Daniel smirked like he had won and I thought about that tennis player that always comes second in Wimbledon, and for some reason that made me cross. My heart growled in my chest like an angry dog.

What a loser Daniel shouted so that everyone in the classroom could hear. I sat down next to Sunya and waited to see if she would glare at him or say something back. She shrank into her chair as though she was trying to hide. She didn't even

173

look in my direction. I wanted to ask if she'd read my special card. I wanted to ask if she'd seen the snowman that looked like her and the snowman that looked like me and if it had made her laugh. I wanted to ask why she hadn't come to the talent contest, and I wanted to tell her all about it, how Jas had been brilliant and how I'd been brave enough to sing and dance on stage. But then I remembered that night in her garden and how she'd said *My mum thinks you are bad news*. So I didn't say any of it. I just stared at my pencil case while Mrs Farmer did the register.

First we did English and we had to write about Our Fabulous Christmas and try to use paragraphs. Nothing fabulous had happened but I didn't want to lie. So I told the truth. I wrote about the football sock full of all the things that Jas had bought me. I described the chicken sandwiches and microwave chips and the chocolates that we ate. I explained that the best bit was when we'd sung Christmas carols at the top of our voices. And at the end I wrote *It wasn't exactly a fabulous Christmas but it was good 'cos I was with Jas*. It was my best piece of writing yet. When I read it out, Mrs Farmer said *That was an excellent piece of work* and my ladybird hopped onto leaf one. The angels had been replaced over Christmas.

After English we did Maths and after Maths we had Assembly. The Headmaster told us that the Ofsted Inspectors had given the school a grade and it was Satisfactory, which meant that we were doing okay but not brilliant. He said we would have got a Good but there was An Incident that upset one of the Inspectors. Mrs Farmer looked at Daniel and shook her head. Daniel's chin slumped onto his knees. There was a flash in my direction. I looked up. Sunya caught my eye and for a millisecond I thought she was going to giggle. But then she turned away and nodded her head a few times as though she was really listening to the Headmaster's talk on New Years' Resolutions. He said *Aim high this year and give yourself a challenge. Don't just make a boring resolution like I must stop biting my nails, or I must stop sucking my thumb.* Everyone started to laugh. The Headmaster smiled and waited for silence. *Set a target that excites you. Even frightens you a bit.* I knew what mine was straightaway.

At playtime I couldn't find Sunya. I waited on our bench and I looked around the playground and I went through the secret door but she wasn't in the storeroom. She must have been in the toilets hiding from Daniel 'cos she was scared. The dog in my chest growled louder than ever. We all went inside and we did History and Geography but I couldn't concentrate. I kept trying to look inside Sunya's pencil case to see if I could spot the Blu-Tack ring. I was wearing mine and I tapped the white stone on the table a few times to try and get her attention. Sunya didn't look up from her books.

At lunchtime I didn't hurry outside 'cos I hate standing by myself. I missed Roger too much to eat my sandwiches so I went to the toilet and played that game where the hand dryer is a fire-breathing monster. I was just taking it and taking it and being tough and I didn't even scream when the flames burned off my skin and made my bones go all black.

I heard a voice outside. Not in the game but in real life. It was shouting. It was spiteful. And the words it said were *Curry Germs.* I looked out of the

175

window. Daniel was following Sunya, yelling things at her back as she tried to walk away. He was with Ryan and Maisie and Alexandra and they were laughing and cheering him on. He shouted *You stink* and *Curry Breath* and *Why do you wear that stupid thing on your head.* He touched the hijab. Actually tried to pull it off. That's when my heart roared. Louder than a dog. Louder than the fire-breathing monster in the toilets. Louder, even, than the silver lion in the sky.

The noise of it vibrated in my head and in my hands and in my legs. I didn't even realise I was running until the door smashed against the tiles and I'd left the bathroom and was halfway down the corridor. I charged outside and screamed *Leave her alone*. People started to laugh. I didn't care. I looked one way, then the other, searching for Sunya. I spotted her in the middle of the playground, her hands on her hijab, trying to stop Daniel from showing her secret hair to the whole school.

LEAVE HER ALONE.

Daniel spun around. He saw me and his lips stretched into a nasty smile. *Come to save Curry Germs* he said. He pulled up his sleeves to fight. Ryan looked fierce. I skidded to a stop and waited for my mouth to say *Yeah I have come to save her,* or *Get out of my way,* or something else that sounded brave. Nothing came out. I waited for my legs to walk forward so I could kick Daniel, but they were paralysed. More and more children were gathering around in a circle, everyone's eyes on me.

You're a loser Daniel said and everyone said things like *Yeah* and *What a gay boy.* And they were right. I took a step backwards. I didn't want to get my head kicked in. It hurt too much last time.

Daniel turned back to Sunya. He grabbed the hijab with his fat fingers. Sunya started to cry. The crowd chanted *Off off off off*.

It reminded me of something. Of being on stage. Of the audience at the talent show.

I wasn't in the playground any more. I was in the theatre, watching Jas. And those words, the words of her song, thundered through my veins.

The playground came back in full sound and full colour. Sunya was sobbing. The hijab was half off. The crowd were cheering. Daniel was laughing. And I was letting him.

NO.

I shouted it as loud as I could. Screamed it. *NO.* Daniel turned around in surprise. I pulled back my fist. Daniel's jaw dropped. I charged at him with all the anger that I'd ever felt. His eyes widened in fear. And when my knuckles hit his nose, Daniel collapsed on the floor. I hit him again, even harder, my fist smacking against his cheek. Sunya looked up. Stared at me in amazement. I kicked Daniel three times and each time my foot crunched against his bones I said a different word. *LEAVE. HER. ALONE.*

Ryan ran off. The crowd backed away. They were scared. Daniel was lying on the floor with his hands over his face. He was crying. I could have kicked him again. I could have stamped on him, or elbowed him, or thumped him in the stomach. But I didn't want to. I didn't need to. I'd just won my Wimbledon. The fat dinner lady blew the whistle.

23

Mrs Farmer sent me to the Headmaster but it was worth it and I only missed a bit of History. When it was time to go home, I got my coat and four people said *Bye*. They'd never talked to me before. I said *Goodbye* and they said *See you later* and one boy asked *You coming to football training tomorrow*. I nodded my head really fast. *Definitely* I replied and he said *Cool*. Daniel heard all this but kept quiet. He didn't even dare look at me. His nose had stopped bleeding but it was bruised. And his cheeks were red 'cos he'd been crying all afternoon. Tears had dripped all over his fractions, smudging the answers.

I only did four questions in Maths. I felt all light and fizzy, lemonade in my veins, and my thoughts popped and bubbled in my brain. My leg kept twitching and it brushed against Sunya's five times in one hour. Three times by accident. Twice on purpose. She didn't say *Stop it*, or *Your leg is bad news*, or anything like that. She just gazed at the fractions and bit the top of her pen and I got the feeling she was trying not to smile.

I walked out of school and the sky was turquoise and there was a massive golden sun. It looked like a huge beach ball floating on a perfect blue sea. I hoped the sun was strong enough to shine right underground. I hoped Roger could feel it all warm on his body. I hoped he wasn't scared or lonely in his grave. I had a sharp pain in my chest then, like indigestion when you've eaten too many slices of pizza at one of those All-You-Can-Eat things. I leaned against a wall and put a hand on my heart and waited for it to pass. It faded to a dull ache but it didn't go away.

I heard footsteps and the tinkle of metal. I turned my head to see Sunya running towards me. *Walking off without saying goodbye* she said, putting her hands on her hips. The sparkle was back and it was brighter than ever. Her hijab was brilliant yellow and her teeth were dazzling white and her eyes shone with the strength of a million suns. She climbed onto the wall and sat next to me and crossed her legs and I just stared at her as though she was a nice view, or a good painting, or an interesting display on the classroom wall. The freckle above her lip jumped about 'cos she was talking. *Walking off without letting me say thank you.* I bit the inside of my cheeks to keep from smiling. *Thank you* I asked, as if I had no idea what she was talking about. *For what.* She leaned forward and put her chin on her hand. That's when I noticed the thin blue circle wrapped around her middle finger.

If envy is red and doubt is black then happiness is brown. I looked from the little brown stone to the tiny brown freckle to her huge brown eyes. *For saving me* she replied as I tried to act cool. *For smashing Daniel's face in.* She was wearing the Blu-Tack ring. She was actually wearing the Blu-Tack ring. Sunya was my friend. *It was nothing* I said. *It was amazing* Sunya replied and she started to laugh. And the thing about Sunya is, once she starts, she just can't stop, and it makes you laugh too. *Don't thank me, Girl M* I said, my sides aching and my smile bigger than a banana. *Thank Spider-Man.* Sunya put her hand on my shoulder and stopped giggling. *You were better than Spider-Man*

179

she whispered in my ear.

It was too hot and there wasn't enough air. I looked at the snow melting on the ground and it was suddenly dead interesting and Very Important to kick it with my foot loads of times. *I'll walk back with you* she said. She stood up on the wall and jumped really high and landed by my side. *Your mum* I said, looking all around in case she was watching. *She said I'm bad news.* Sunya linked my arm and grinned. *Mums and dads don't know anything.*

On the way back, I told Sunya about Roger. *I'm so sorry* she said. *He was a nice cat.* She'd never met him but it didn't matter. Roger was a nice cat. The nicest cat. Everyone knew that. We bumped into the old man with the flat cap. Fred wagged his tail and licked my hand. It left a trail of sticky spit but I didn't mind. *You okay, lad* the old man asked, sucking his pipe. The smoke smelled like Bonfire Night. *How're you feeling.* I shrugged. *I understand* the old man replied seriously. *I lost my old dog Pip last year and it still hurts now. Got this rascal four months ago* he went on, pointing at Fred. *Damn hard work he is.* Fred jumped up and put his paws on my tummy. *Seems to like you though* the old man said, scratching his head with the end of his pipe as if he was thinking. *Now here's an idea. Why don't you come and give me a hand with young Fred. You can help me walk him.* I stroked Fred's grey ears. *That would be the best thing ever* I said and the old man grinned. *Good. Good. I live in that house over there.* He pointed at a white building a few metres away. *Make sure you ask your mother* he said. *I haven't got a proper mum* I replied. *But I'll ask Dad.* The old man patted my head. *You do that, lad* he said. *Down, Fred.* Fred ignored him so I grabbed his feet and pushed him off gently. His paws were fat and squishy. The old man clipped a lead on Fred's collar and hobbled off down the road, waving his pipe to say goodbye. *I'll come too* Sunya said as we started walking again. *I'll bring Sammy and we will have adventures.*

We stopped at a shop. Sunya wanted to buy something for Roger. She only had fifty pence, so she bought a small red flower. When she paid, I saw something brown and fluffy on the counter. It gave me an idea. I got out my birthday money from Granny.

The cottage drive was empty. Dad's car wasn't there. I should've felt guilty that I was letting a Muslim near our house when he was at the building site. But I didn't. Sunya's mum doesn't like me. Dad doesn't like Sunya. But just 'cos they're grown-ups, doesn't mean they're always right.

That's where Roger's buried I said, pointing to a rectangle of fresh mud in the back garden. *Just under there.* Sunya knelt down and touched the grave. *He was a lovely cat.* I crouched down. *The loveliest cat* I replied. She held out her hand and looked at the ring on her middle finger. *There's something you don't know* she said in this low voice that gave me goose bumps. *About the rings.* I stared at the little brown stone. *What* I asked. *What about them.* Sunya looked all around the garden to make sure no one was listening, then grabbed my t-shirt and pulled me close. *They can bring things back to life* she whispered. I didn't speak though I had a billion questions. *But only at night time. If we put the stones together on top of Roger's grave, when the clock strikes twelve, he will have the power to climb*

181

out of the ground and catch mice and play in the garden. I started to smile. *Will he come and see me* I asked. *Of course* Sunya said. *That is part of the magic. He'll jump right through your window and lie next to you and purr. He'll be all warm and furry but he'll disappear when you wake up. He'll go back to his underground bed and he'll sleep all day so that he has lots of energy for his next midnight adventure.*

It wasn't true but it didn't matter. It made me feel better. Sunya took off her Blu-Tack ring and pulled mine off my finger. Then she pressed the white stone and the brown stone together as I dug a little hole in the grave. She kissed the rings and then I kissed the rings and we dropped them on the grave. We covered them up with mud and snow and our fingers touched four times. Sunya laid the red flower on top. *Roger is a magic cat now* she said and the pain in my chest faded a little bit.

There was a knock at the window. I jumped up and stood in front of Sunya, scared it was Dad, but it was just Jas, home from school. Next to her pink head was a bright green one. Jas smiled happily and waved at Sunya, who peered around my legs and waved back. Jas pulled Leo by the hand and dragged him into the lounge, kissing him on the lips before they disappeared through the door.

The garden suddenly felt too small. There was nowhere to look and my arms felt clumsy and I was very aware of Sunya's body near my legs. *I should go* she said, climbing to her feet but not meeting my eyes. Her hands and knees were wet through. *My mum'll kill me if I'm back too late.*

So much had happened that day, it felt strange saying goodbye. I didn't want her to leave. Sunya wiped her fingers on her thighs and held out her hand. *Friends forever* she asked, her voice a bit higher than normal. *Friends forever* I replied. We shook hands quickly, my palm hot against hers. When we let go, we glanced at each other, and then looked away.

I focused on a robin that was sitting on a branch. Its chest was red and its wings were brown and its beak was open and it was singing as if—

Jamie.

I jumped. Sunya smiled. Her hands moved up to her head. Brown fingers curled around the yellow material.

She pulled the hijab down.

Forehead.

Hair.

Straight shiny hair that fell all the way to her shoulders in a black silk curtain.

She blinked shyly. I moved closer. She was even prettier without the scarf. I looked at Sunya, really looked at her, trying to take everything in. Then I zoomed forward and kissed her freckle, and it was exciting and frightening, just like the Headmaster had said our resolution should be.

Sunya gasped and ran off, her perfect hair swishing in the wind. *See you tomorrow* she called over her shoulder, looking back one last time. I was worried I'd scared her but she touched the freckle and grinned and blew a kiss right at my face. Her eyes twinkled more than diamonds and I felt like the luckiest, richest boy on the planet.

I went inside and climbed the stairs and stared in the mirror. I was too big for the Spider-Man t-shirt. I pulled it over my head and threw it on the floor and checked my reflection. The superhero had disappeared. In his place stood a boy. In his place stood Jamie Matthews. I had a shower and put on a pair of pyjamas.

*   *   *

Dad got home at six. He made beans on toast. We ate it in front of the TV and he asked about our days. *Fine* I said and *Okay* Jas replied. She wouldn't say anything about Sunya and I wouldn't say anything about Leo. It was nice to have a secret. Jas only had two bites of toast and Dad had three beers. If Ofsted inspected my family then I know what grade we'd get. Satisfactory. Okay but not brilliant. But that's fine by me.

Much later, I went into Jas's room, something hidden behind my back. She was painting her fingernails black and listening to music. There were lots of guitars and screaming and shouting. *What do you want* she said, wiggling her hands in the air to make them dry. *You sent the t-shirt, didn't you* I asked. Her hands stopped moving and she looked worried. *It's okay* I said. *I don't mind.* She blew on her fingers. *Yeah. Sorry. I just didn't want you to think Mum had forgotten.* I sat on her bed. *It was a good present.* She dipped the brush in the black pot. *You don't mind that it wasn't from Mum* she asked, painting her little finger. *I like it better 'cos it's from you* I replied. *I got you this.* I held out the brown, fluffy bear. *To replace Burt. I pulled his eyes off and everything.*

Jas put the new Burt on her lap, careful not to get polish on his fur. I stretched from the mattress to the stereo and stopped the music. *I want to tell you something* I said. *Something important.* Jas stroked Burt's fur. *You know the song you sang on stage.* She

184

nodded slowly. *That's exactly how I feel about you.* Jas blinked back tears. The nail polish must have been really strong to make her eyes water. *Your strength gives me the courage to fly* I sang badly and Jas elbowed me in the ribs. *Get out of my room, you sickly little bastard* she said. But she was smiling.

And so was I.

ACKNOWLEDGEMENTS

This novel started out as a simple idea and a few scribbles on a notepad. Without the help of some important people, it would never have turned into the book in your hands.

Thanks to Jackie Head, who picked *My Sister Lives on the Mantelpiece* out of the slush pile and changed my life one day with a phone call. Warmest thanks to my agent, Catherine Clarke, for guiding me with such wisdom and intelligence. To all the team at Orion, thank you for doing such a great job and for getting so many people excited about my book. And a special thanks to my editor, Fiona Kennedy, for treating the manuscript with such understanding and respect while drawing the very best out of the story.

Above all, thanks to my family and friends, who were there before the book and will be there long after it. In particular, I am indebted to my brother and sisters, my mum and dad and my wonderful husband. Much like Sunya, you make life sparkle.

Annabel Pitcher
West Yorkshire
July 2010